Unexpected Love

Love Stings Series, Book 4

By Evan Grace

Unexpected Love

Limitless Publishing, LLC
Kailua, HI 96734
www.limitlesspublishing.com

Formatting: Limitless Publishing

ISBN-13: 978-1-64034-143-2
ISBN-10: 1-64034-143-9

Dedication

This is for anyone who has fallen in love.

Author's Note:

Chloe and her brother, Carter, are the adopted children of Ian and Garrett. I decided to have them refer to their dad, Ian, as Dad and refer to Garrett as Pops. They share a lot of scenes together, and I knew it could get real confusing real quick.

Prologue

Joe

I take a sip of my beer while I watch my cousin/best friend, Violet, be danced around the floor by her new husband. Shit, I can't believe she's married. Hell, I can't believe she's married to someone twelve years older, but he makes her happy and seems like a good guy. As long as she's happy, I'll keep my trap shut.

I reach up and loosen up my tie. Violet's lucky. I love her and said yes when she asked me to be her Man of Honor. I figured she would've had one of her sisters or Abby or Carrington, but I'm only days older than her, and growing up, she and I were more like brother and sister than cousins.

I feel someone standing next to me and turn to find my mom as she wraps her arms around my waist, so I wrap my arm around her shoulders.

"You look so handsome in your tux. It was a beautiful ceremony, wasn't it?"

"Thanks, Mom. Yeah it was, and it was the kind

1

I like—short and sweet." I bend down to kiss her forehead. My mom is a shorty, and I'm tall like my dad—hell, I'm taller than him now.

"That Chloe sure is a beautiful singer." Yes, she is, and there's nothing like fighting a hard on standing up in front of a bunch of people, but shit, I've been fighting one since the first time I saw Chloe in a long time. It was after Violet's grandpa passed away and we were at her parents' house. I've never in my life had that kind of reaction to the opposite sex before. I had a body buzz to end all body buzzes, and I knew she felt it too, but I never got the chance to see if anything could happen. She went back to Atlanta before I could make a move.

Yes, Chloe and I share Violet as a cousin, but we're not related. Chloe's my aunt Stacy's cousin on her dad's family's side. I'm related on my dad's side. Over the years, we've seen each other at some of Aunt Stacy and Uncle Dustin's family parties, but we've never really spent any time together.

"Yeah, she's great." My eyes scan the room, and I find her. She's with both of her dads standing by the bar. Her hair is so dark it's almost black; her skin's like porcelain, but it's her eyes that truly suck me in. They're a cerulean blue and surrounded by dark, thick lashes. I would've thought they were contacts, but her younger brother, Carter, has the same eyes. Chloe must feel my stare, because she turns and looks right at me.

It gives me a thrill that even from across the room, I see her cheeks turn a light shade of pink before she walks away from her parents. I don't know why, but she's been avoiding me all day. I know I can be a little intimidating. Since joining the police force, I've put on quite a bit of muscle and have tattoos on both arms. Add in my height and it makes an intimidating package.

My mom kisses my cheek and then goes to my dad. My feet start carrying me toward Chloe when my nephew Dalton comes running toward me. "Hey, little man." I pick him up and kiss his chubby cheek.

He starts babbling in his secret toddler language that I don't understand at all. My eyes find her again, and she's watching us with a small smile on her lips. We head right to her, and this time she doesn't run. Of course, she acknowledges little man first. "Hey buddy. Aren't you just the cutest?"

"Thanks," I tell her with a smirk.

"Haha. You're such a funny guy." Dalton squirms in my arms, so I set him down and he runs right to my mom. I shake my head because my parents spoil Abby's kids rotten, but I love it—I love how happy my sister is. It's hard to believe that it was so long ago that we almost lost Abby, but now she's married with three kids and so incredibly happy. Her husband and I work together on the police force, and he's become a good friend.

I grab her hand. "Dance with me?"

She wants to say no, I can tell, but I don't give her the chance. I pull her out to the dance floor and begin swaying to the music. Her body feels so good pressed up against mine. In her heels she comes up to my nose, but without them I know she barely comes to my chin. Her tits are high and firm, and in the dress she's wearing, I'm getting a prime view of her cleavage. She's thin but soft, with enough curves highlighted in her silky blue dress to make my dick hard.

She smells like flowers and sunshine, and her skin looks so soft and smooth. "You look beautiful."

"You're not so bad yourself. The toast you gave was really sweet."

"I don't think anything I've ever done has been classified as sweet." I pull her a little closer, not even caring that she can probably tell my cock's half hard, but it's her fault.

"Please, I saw you with your nephews earlier. They use you like their own personal jungle gym. You just smiled and let them do it. Last night during the rehearsal dinner, it wasn't lost on me that your niece sat with you and you guys were coloring for a while." Her pearly white smile puts an ache in my chest that is completely unfamiliar to me.

"It's nice to know that you've noticed me."

***

I strip out of my shirt and throw it on the chair in my hotel room. My brother, Parker, wanted to share a room with me, but in the off chance I brought a woman back to my room, I told him to fuck off and to room with our cousin Luke. Unfortunately, I'm here alone with only the images of Chloe to keep me company. I could've gone to a bar to pick up a woman for the night if I wanted to—I've never had trouble finding a willing woman—but I just don't feel like it. Strange.

A knock on the door pulls me out of my thoughts. I look through the peephole and find the last person I expected to see on the other side of my door: Chloe. When I open it, she stands there in that fucking dress that turns me on like nothing else.

"Hey." Fuck, I love her sexy, raspy voice.

"What are you doing here?" I stand back and watch her as she steps inside my room. Her sweet scent follows her in. My eyes drift to the back of her dress, and my dick immediately gets hard. The fabric hugs her heart-shaped ass, and all I want to do is grab it.

She stops in the middle of my room, and I let the door shut with a quiet snick. Silence surrounds us, and I'm wondering what's happening. When Chloe finally turns around, she stuns me. She slips her dress off, and I watch in utter fascination as it slides down her delicious body. She saunters toward me until we're almost touching.

My mouth salivates as my eyes rake over her body. It's even better in just teeny, tiny panties. Her hands slide up my chest until they wind around my neck. "I want you to fuck me."

"You want me to fuck you?" She doesn't know how badly I want to.

"Yes. I want you to use," she palms my hard cock through my dress pants, "this. I want you to make me come."

I don't think she knows what she's asking. I have a tendency to be a little rough, a little intense. I'm not sure if I can rein it in, not with her, and that is what I tell her. "Baby, I don't think you could handle this ride."

Her lips quirk, and she trails her hand to the button of my pants. With a quick flick of her fingers, they're undone and my zipper is down. I should stop her, but I'm dying to know what she is going to do next. Chloe doesn't disappoint when she reaches inside my pants, wrapping her hand around my cock…or at least trying to. My size can sometimes be a problem.

Chloe's eyes widen comically before she bites her lip and then licks them. I swear my cock pulses in her hand. A drop of come beads at the tip, and she swipes her thumb across it before bringing it up to her mouth and sucking it in. She does this sexy little moan. "You taste good." A groan slips past my lips.

I should send her on her way and tell her I'm not interested, but I am. Right now I want her so bad I can taste it. My blood is pumping hard through my veins, my cock is leaking, and my body is strung tight.

***

Chloe

I shouldn't be here right now—I'm too old for him. Hell, I held him when he was a toddler. I've heard stories about him, and I know he's a ladies man. But to be honest, I need a self-esteem boost. A year ago, I was dating Teddy—a total douche bag, but I looked past that because he was gorgeous and good in bed. That was until I found him out at a club one night, two other women hanging on him, and overheard him talk about how frigid I was in bed. They all laughed at my expense. I didn't bother confronting him because I was humiliated.

I'd snapped a picture of the three of them, and in the parking lot I texted it to him with a big "Fuck You" attached. Then I went to my brother's, where I got drunk on Jack Daniel's and then passed right the fuck out. I haven't been with a man since then, and I just need to know if it's true what he said.

I grab his hand and bring it to my mouth, sucking a finger in. He groans, and I feel my panties get damp. His cornflower blue eyes darken. I pull his finger from my mouth, take his hand, and place it between my legs. He sucks in a breath, and I know it's because he can feel how wet I am through my panties. I press his fingers against my clit and move them slowly, moaning because it feels so exquisite.

He holds my stare as I feel his fingers move under the gusset of my panties, sliding through my wetness. My eyes start to close. "Keep them open," he growls. They pop back open, and goosebumps break out all over my body. A shiver wracks my body as he pushes one finger inside of me. My head falls back, and I moan loud and long.

Joe finally bends down, and his lips are on mine. I open to him immediately, welcoming his tongue to duel with mine. It's quite clear that he can kiss. His tongue strokes mine, and between that, his finger in my pussy, and my dry spell, I feel like I'm going to come and soon.

I let go of Joe's hand as he pulls his finger out of me and then pushes two back inside. A groan slips from my lips right into his mouth. My hands wind around the back of his head, and I sink further into the kiss. "You're so fucking wet for me," he whispers. "Are you going to come for me like a good girl?"

My channel spasms around his fingers, and it's his turn to groan against my lips. He curls his fingers inside of me, and he rubs circles around my clit with his thumb. The orgasm hits me hard. Pulling my mouth from his, I cry out. "That's it, give it to me." A squelching sound fills the room, and I know it's because I get really, really wet when I come.

Joe pulls his fingers from my spasming core and brings them to his lips. His tongue lashes out, licking and sucking the soaked digits. I swear just watching him I have a mini-orgasm. He pulls them from his mouth, and his lips curl up in the corners. "Now I'm going to fuck you."

It happens so fast. I fly through the air, and my back hits the wall. My legs automatically wrap around his hips. I hear the unmistakable sound of material ripping, and then my panties are gone. His lips are suddenly on mine, his tongue in my mouth, and we're coming together in a gnashing of teeth and flesh.

One hand disappears, and he presses into me harder against the wall. Then I hear the crinkle of the condom wrapper, and then his hips pull back from me. "Pull me out." I reach between us and drag his zipper down. I reach inside, freeing him from his pants. After taking the condom from him, I slowly sheath him, wishing I could see it better because I'm sure it's a thing of beauty.

He lines up his cock with my entrance. "Are you ready for me?" His voice is laced with lust.

"Yes," I whisper. His lips hit mine again before thrusting inside me deep and hard. I cry out because it's that fine line between pleasure and pain. He doesn't move, giving me time to adjust to the intrusion. An ache starts deep inside me, and I need him to move. "Please."

"Please what?" he whispers against my lips.

"I need you to fuck me." That's all he needs to hear before he pulls almost all the way out and then thrusts back inside. "Yes," I cry out.

His lips move to my neck. "You feel so good, baby. So tight...so wet...warm." The sounds of slapping flesh fill the room, and my eyes roll as he kisses and sucks on the sensitive skin of my neck.

It doesn't take long before that feeling below starts to build and I'm close to coming. Joe's lips move until they're back on mine. We're not kissing—our lips are merely touching, our breaths mingling. My head flies back, banging into the wall as I come and harder than before.

I keep coming as we're moving. My back hits the bed, and he begins thrusting into me at a punishing pace. I cry out with each thrust until finally he plants himself to the root and groans against my lips.

Our panting breaths fan against each other's cheeks. I let my hands drift lightly up and down his back. He pushes up and looks down at me. "I didn't hurt you, did I?"

I shake my head. "No, you didn't."

He touches his lips to mine. "Good." I whimper as he pulls out of me and gets up and disappears into the bathroom.

I ease off the bed, already sore between my legs, but I don't care. It'll be nice to have that reminder, and now I have the validation that I'm not cold in bed. I pick up my dress off the floor, but before I can get it on, it's being yanked out of my hands. Joe turns me around to face him, and I can't help but check out his amazing body. He's lean but muscular, his arms are covered in ink, and he's got that v-cut under his abs that makes women do crazy things. None of it compares to his cock. It's long and thick, and my mouth waters to taste it.

He raises an eyebrow, and I sink to my knees. I grab his cock in my hand and drag my tongue up the underside of it. It starts getting hard again. Slowly I work him over until he's completely hard. My tongue swirls around the tip before sucking him deep. My lips are stretched tight around his length. I reach down, grab his balls in my other hand, and massage them.

There is a bite of pain as he spears his fingers through my hair and begins fucking my mouth. His urgent grunts and groans are music to my ears. "I'm gonna come," he says, warning me, but I continue sucking. The first splash of come on my tongue is warm and salty, and I moan at the taste. He keeps coming until he finally pulls his softening cock from my mouth.

Joe lifts me up to my feet and then kisses my lips, unconcerned about the fact I just had his come in my mouth. His tongue snakes inside, and my arms wind around his neck. I feel us moving until I'm flat on my back and he's half on me and half on the bed. "Stay with me tonight," he tells me.

"Okay." Joe situates us, my back firmly against his front. His arms wrap around me tight, and it doesn't take long before my eyes drift shut.

***

My eyes flutter open as sunlight peeks through the opening in the curtains. Joe's arm is still wrapped around me, hugging me close. Carefully, I pull his arm up and slide out of the bed. The bedside clock say it's seven in the morning, so I've had a total of three hours of sleep, and I have to be at the airport in two hours.

The ache between my legs is going to be a reminder of the amazing night I had. Joe woke me up shortly after I'd fallen asleep after his blowjob, and he ate my pussy until I came all over his face. Then he'd fucked me so hard that when I came I almost passed out.

I watch him sleep as I slip my dress and heels back on. Quietly, I move to the door, even though I feel guilty about leaving like this. Of course, knowing his reputation, he'll probably be grateful that he doesn't have to kick me out of his bed.

I open the door slowly and quietly back out of his room, letting the door shut as soft as possible. I turn around and let out a scream but quickly cover my mouth.

Fuck…My…Life! I stare at my pops; my brother, Carter; my older cousin Stacy, who I call

Tay Tay; her husband, Dustin, who is also Joe's uncle; and Violet's parents. I'm a grown woman, but right now I feel like I'm fifteen again and getting caught sneaking out to meet a boy. In my head, I chant over and over: *be cool, be cool.*

"Good morning! How're y'all doing? I'm just going to grab a coffee downstairs. Does anyone want one?" Before they can answer, I hustle down the hall to my room and quickly slip my keycard in the door. When it turns green, I open it and escape inside. Carter slips through the door before it closes.

"The walk of shame? Seriously?" He chuckles before he plops down on my bed.

"Oh, shut the hell up." I sit down next to him and bury my face in my hands. "That was so humiliating. What are you doing up so early?" My brother is one of my best friends, even though he's three years younger than I am.

"Dad woke me and Pops up, so we left him to snore in peace and we had breakfast."

I rest my head on Carter's shoulder. "I'm so stupid. I slept with Joe."

"Violet's cousin Joe?" He bumps me with his shoulder. "Get 'em, you cradle robber."

Around anyone else, my brother doesn't say much, and right about now I wish it was true with me, too. "Shut your pie hole. It was stupid, I know it, but ugh…I'm not talking to you about this."

"Good. I don't want to hear about my sister's sex life. My stomach is turning just at the thought. You better get ready. We'll have to get you to the airport in two hours."

I unfortunately can't stay. I wasn't able to get

anyone to cover my shift on Monday, and one of my co-workers is always trying to get me fired, so I can't push it. Who knows what she'd try to do?

For the past six years, I've worked at Harmon Jewelry, a family-run business. I started out in retail, and then my boss saw my design book and had me make a couple of pieces; he hired me as a designer right on the spot. Hailey is the other designer, and she's always been jealous of me. It's not my fault my sales are better than hers—I'm just always able to capture the look that the client wants.

"I hate that I'm missing brunch and presents. Fucking Hailey!" I climb off the bed, grab my stuff, and head into the bathroom. After a quick shower, I pull the rubber band out of my hair and brush it out before throwing it back up. I skip makeup and just moisturize and brush my teeth.

I throw on jean shorts and a tank top. I slip my feet into my black Adidas and tie my cardigan around my waist. After shoving everything into my bag, I step back into my room and find Carter gone and Joe standing in the middle of the room with two cups of coffee.

He holds one out to me. "Your brother said you'd need this."

I take it from him. "Thanks. What are you doing here?"

His deep voice rumbles. "I woke up and you were gone. I ran into your dad in the hall, and he said you were getting ready to head to the airport. I'm here to offer my services." I take a sip from my coffee cup.

"You want to take me to the airport? Why?"

"Why not? Maybe I'm just a nice guy and want to spend a little more time with you before you go."

Wow, I was not expecting that. "Okay, sure."

I move through the room and make sure I have everything. Joe doesn't say anything, but I can feel his eyes on me as I move throughout the suddenly small space. His woodsy scent fills my nose, and pieces of the night before flash through my mind, making my nipples tingle. He's got the kind of stamina that I thought was only possible in romance novels.

Slinging my bag over my shoulder, I pick my coffee up off the table. "I'm ready."

Joe, being the gentleman, takes my bag from me. He holds the door open for me, so I pass by and step out into the hall. In companionable silence, we walk side by side to the elevator and ride down to the lobby.

My dad is waiting to get on the elevator when the doors open. "Hey, Dad." He wraps his arms around me, hugging me tight.

"Hey, honey. I can't believe you can't stay for the rest of the festivities. Fuck Hailey." He's heard me say "fuck Hailey" enough that he and Pops have both said it to me. It's now a running joke.

With a laugh, I wrap my arms around him. "I know, but it's okay—I need to get home to Ragnar and Lagertha." I'm a total *Vikings* nerd and named my cats after my two favorite people.

"You and those damn furballs. I want you to call us as soon as you're home. Your dad's outside having a cigarette. Make sure you give him hell when you say goodbye." He kisses my forehead. "I love you, munchkin."

"I love you, Daddy." I walk toward the doors outside and hear Joe say goodbye to my dad. Sure enough, when I step through the doors, I find my pops smoking a cigarette. Over the years he's smoked on and off, but it was only after my uncle Gary's death that he started up again. That's why Dad never says anything, because Uncle Gary and Pops were really close and it hit him really hard.

"Hey, Papa. I'm getting ready to leave."

He puts his cigarette out and wraps me in a hug. "I hate that you're leaving already." He looks over my shoulder, and I know he's looking at Joe. Leaning in close to my ear, he whispers, "I believe there's a story I need to hear there."

"Hmmm…maybe. I love you. I already promised Dad that I'd call when I get home."

"Good girl. Be safe, and Joe, I expect you to get my daughter to the airport safely."

Joe comes up next to me and holds his hand out. "You bet, Mr. Hutchins."

"Your dads are both great," Joe says as we pull out of the parking lot. "How old were you when they adopted you?"

"I was almost four, and Carter was almost one." I lean my head back on my seat because honestly I'm exhausted and I don't want to talk about a past I vaguely remember. "I still can't believe Vi is married now. Diego is a good guy, and he can put up with our crazy families."

"I thought mine was crazy until I met yours." Out of the corner of my eye, I watch him look at me and smile. *God, he's got a great smile*. I can see why he has no problem getting into a woman's panties, present company included.

"They are pretty crazy, but I love them. Things have slowly started to get back to normal since Uncle Gary died. Fuck, that was hard on everyone. I still can't believe it. My pops was the baby, and Uncle Gary really took him under his wing when they were growing up." My nose begins to burn, and my eyes begin to mist over.

Joe surprises me by placing his hand on mine. I continue to stare out the window, but I squeeze his back.

When we reach the airport, I'm slightly disappointed. I wanted more time with him, but why?

Joe pulls the car up to the entrance, grabs my bag out of the back, and comes around to my side. He stops right in front of me, reaching out and stroking my cheek with his thumb. "I had a great time last night. Can I look you up if I'm in Atlanta?"

My belly warms at the thought. "Yeah, that'd be nice." He leans down, kissing me slowly and thoroughly, but all too soon he pulls back.

"All right, baby, have a safe flight." I give him a smile before pulling away and heading inside the airport, knowing I'll probably never see him again unless it's because our families get together. Oh, well...tomorrow he'll be on to the next girl and I'll be forgotten.

Chapter One

Chloe

Eight Weeks Later

"You've got to be joking. *Please* tell me you read the test wrong." I stare at my doctor, praying that she's wrong, that her test was wrong. In my heart, though, I know she's not.

"Chloe, I take it this wasn't a planned pregnancy. Do we need to discuss options?"

I stare at her before looking at my lap. "I don't know. God, does that sound terrible or what?" But in my heart, I know that's not true. My eyes lift to find hers. "I'm thirty-one years old. I'm single, with no prospects in sight. This may be my only chance to be a mother." After a dramatic pause, I whisper, "No, I guess I don't."

She gives me a kind smile. "Okay. We'll get you a prescription for prenatal vitamins, and I want you to get some blood work done. We'll see you back in a month, and we'll see if we can hear the heartbeat."

17

My heart beats rapidly, and butterflies flutter around in my stomach. I've had no symptoms other than zero periods and my breasts being super tender—almost to the point that I've had a hard time wearing bras. Well, and the smell of chicken makes me queasy. Two weeks ago, I suspected that I was pregnant, but I chose to ignore it, hoping I was wrong.

I haven't seen or heard from Joe since our night together, but I'm not surprised. I knew what I was getting when I slept with him, and that's the way I wanted it with him. I knew it would be easy and uncomplicated, but of course now things have gotten *very* complicated. We used condoms—a lot of them—so I'm not sure if one was compromised or what.

Am I going to tell him that he's going to be a father? Of course I'm going to tell him, but if he doesn't seem interested in co-parenting with me, then that'll be that, I guess. *Oh God*, I have to tell my dads. Dad will be great and excited about being a grandpa. Pops, on the other hand, will try to drive down to Beaufort so he can kick Joe's ass, but he'll be excited about a baby, and Carter will support me however I need him to.

I stop at reception on my way out and schedule my next appointment. They give me the lab requisition form so I can get blood work done. When I step outside, the hot sun beats down on me. I slip my shades on and head to my beautiful royal blue Chevy Camaro that I'm going to have to trade in for something with four doors. I let my hand trail over the blue paint and remember when I bought it.

It was when I turned twenty-eight and I'd just sold two really big jewelry pieces—my boss had given me a huge bonus. Before that, I'd driven a Corolla but had wanted a Camaro so bad. At least I have some time to enjoy him before I trade him in for something else.

My brother is a music teacher at the junior high we went to, so I head toward the school. He should be done by now, but I know he always hangs out afterward even when there's no band practice. I can sing and play piano, but when he touches any instrument, it's like he can play it immediately.

Carter's never been much of a talker unless it's with family, but he seems to communicate through music. During my freshman year of high school, he wrote me the most beautiful song to sing at the talent show. He was eleven at the time. Carter has a gift that so many would kill for, and I love watching him create his musical pieces.

We're adopted, and neither of us remembers our biological parents, so we have no idea if they were musicians or what. Our pops and his brothers and our cousins are all musicians, and it was just natural for us to be involved, too.

Dad's the only one who doesn't play or sing. Oh sure, he tries, but it's not pretty.

In the parking lot of the school, I pull out my phone and send Carter a quick text.

Chloe: Hey I'm outside. Do you have a minute to talk?

He answers me almost immediately.

19

Carter: Sure, I'll be right down.

I stand outside the locked doors and stare out at nothing. My mind is a million miles away, and I jerk when Carter calls my name. I turn to look at him and smile. Carter has the same dark hair that looks almost black and the same cerulean blue eyes. Except his porcelain skin is covered in colorful ink. The school requires him to keep his tattoos covered; he wears a lot of dress shirts with the sleeves rolled up to where his colorful sleeves begin.

"Hey. What's up? You looked like you were somewhere else." I may be older, but that doesn't mean that he hasn't always watched over me.

"Yeah, I'm sorry. I've got a lot on my mind. Are you free to talk?"

"Let's head to my office."

I follow him down the hall until we reach his office, which is just inside the band room. He sits behind his desk, and I smile. He's right at home teaching music, and on the weekends we have our band. We started Beautiful Rage with our best friend/neighbor growing up, Eli. Then Kyle and Robby joined.

"What did you want to talk about?"

Picking at my thumbnail, I take a deep breath. "I'm pregnant."

His eyes widen comically. "Pregnant? Like you're going to have a baby, pregnant?"

"I suspected it, but I found out today." Carter gets up and comes around his desk. He grabs me out of my chair and hugs me tight.

"I'm going to be the best uncle this kid has ever

seen." He sets me back on my feet. "Who's the father?"

"Joe Carmichael."

"Really? Do I need to kick his ass? Are you okay?"

I nod. "Yep, and no you don't need to kick his ass. Am I okay? I think I'm in shock right now. It almost doesn't seem real." I begin to cry, and my brother wraps his arms around me.

"Why are you crying?" Because I was the only girl in a house full of men, they hated it when I'd cry. The first time I had my heart broken, I thought my sweet, loving dad—not my pops, who has an even worse temper—would have to be pulled back into the house to keep him from going after the fourteen-year-old boy who dared to break up with me.

"I'm scared." My voice is soft. "What if I become our birth mom?" Our dads wouldn't tell us a whole lot except that our birth parents were drug addicts, and it was when Carter was born and tested positive for cocaine that Child Protective Services stepped in and took us away.

"Chloe, do you do drugs?" I shake my head. "Then you're not going to become her."

"What if I'm a terrible mom? I never babysat when I was younger, and sure, I'm around our cousins' kids, but I always felt awkward around them, like I don't have that mothering gene."

He pulls back and looks down at me. "That's the craziest thing I've ever heard. When we have family get-togethers, who do the kids flock to? How many times have all of the little ones made you play and

21

sing songs from *Frozen* and *Tangled* to them? You just don't see how good you are with them."

I pull away and wipe the tears from my eyes. "Sorry, I don't know what my problem is." I look him in the eye. "Don't even say it's hormones or I'll punch you in the throat." I'm only half serious, at least about the throat part. "I think I'm just scared about doing this, scared about telling Dad and Pops, and scared to tell *him*. I'm prepared to do this alone if he doesn't want to be involved."

"You have nothing to be scared of, and you're not alone." He hugs me again and then kisses my forehead. "You. Are. Never. Alone."

He walks me out and offers to go with me when I tell our dads. "I'll let you know if I need you there with me," I say.

I head back to my house, and as soon as I step inside, I'm greeted by my babies. Ragnar and Lagertha are Maine Coon cats. They're both silver tabbies with green eyes. My favorite thing about them is that they both have big bushy tails and big old ears that stand straight up.

"Hi, my babies." I pick up Laggie first, cuddling my girl to my chest.

"Meow," she says, cuddling into my neck.

I kiss the top of her head before putting her down and picking up my boy, who always waits patiently for me to finish loving on his sister.

"Come here, my baby." Everyone makes fun of me for the way I talk to my cats, but I don't care—I love them and have had them both since they were kittens. My boy is a moose, so I pick up his lard butt.

Ragnar snuggles into me and purrs, which sounds like a motorboat. "Did you miss me?"

"Meow," he replies.

I put him down, and they follow me into the kitchen of my adorable little bungalow. My whole house is bright with its high white ceilings and glass light fixtures that illuminate the kitchen and dining room. Ceiling fans hang in the other rooms.

The flooring is made from Brazilian teak and tongue hardwood. It's gorgeous and makes it easy to clean up the cat hair. Both cats were declawed before I got them, and honestly I wouldn't have done it had I had them as tiny kittens. The kitchen is all white with stainless steel appliances and white marble countertops.

Ragnar is impatient as always and sits next to where I keep their treats, meowing his impatience. "I hear you, baby." I grab the bag as Lagertha comes over to stand next to her brother. Ragnar lets his sister have the first treat, and my girl takes it right from my fingers. She prances off with her treat, and then my boy swishes his tail back and forth while I grab his. "Meow." He inches closer to me.

After grabbing his treat, he trots off, and I shake my head. *Pig*. I grab a glass of iced tea and my Kindle and step out the back door onto the cute little deck I have. I set my glass and Kindle down and slip off my flip flops, placing them on the empty chair across from me.

My mind drifts off, and my hand goes to my lower abdomen. I still can't believe there is a baby in there. How hard is it going to be to do it alone? I know I can do it, and lots of women do it alone every day.

I still need to tell my parents, and then I need to tell Joe. Picking up my glass of iced tea, I close my eyes and say a little prayer that it goes well.

***

Pulling into the driveway of the home I grew up in, I smile. I have so many great memories here. Carter and I were, and still are, lucky to have two dads that love us fiercely. Have we missed out not having a mom? Not at all, because we have a wonderful grandma and aunts who were there for me when it came to woman stuff when I was growing up.

Don't get me wrong—sometimes we did get shit from people for having two dads. They said that we were gay too and that we were probably getting molested. Carter got it worse, but he just started kicking anyone's ass that messed with him or me. We know families with moms and dads that are completely dysfunctional, and ours isn't perfect, but it's a hell of a lot better than others I've seen.

Our best friend, Eli, grew up in the house right next door. His parents still live there. It was my dads that helped Eli come out to his parents when he was sixteen. It wasn't easy, and Eli and his mom didn't talk for a while, but thankfully she came around.

I reach the front door and give a knock before I open the door. "Dad? Pops?" My dad comes out of the kitchen.

"Hi, baby girl." He wraps me in a hug and squeezes me tight. "You look gorgeous as always." I wrap my arm around his waist as he leads me through the living room and into the kitchen. My dad has a heavy sprinkling of silver hair mixed in with his blond. He and Pops seem to get more and more handsome with age.

Speaking of my pops, we find him at the stove stirring something in a big pot. He gives me a huge smile. "Hi, honey." I move toward him and give him a quick squeeze and a kiss. His gray, shaggy hair is in desperate need of a cut, and he's wearing torn jeans and an old, faded AC/DC t-shirt.

"Hey, Daddy." He's always been able to read me, because he gives me a quizzical look.

"What's wrong?"

Dad comes up behind me and wraps his arms around my shoulders. "Are you okay?"

"I'm fine, okay? Can we eat, and then we can talk?"

My dad kisses my temple. "Whatever you want."

The three of us make chitchat while Pops finishes dinner and Dad sets the table. Dad tries to offer me wine, but I tell him I have to design some pieces so I need to be clearheaded.

"Is Hailey still giving you grief?" Pops asks from his place by the stove.

"Sometimes she's fine, but then sometimes she's the devil. I don't get it; she's really talented, and her pieces are sought after too." It's true: Hailey in my eyes is really talented...she's just got a shitty attitude.

"Well, Mr. Harmon better do something if she

starts shit with you again, or I'll come down there and have a talk with her," Pops says as he and Dad carry bowls and a plate to the table.

I grab a marinated chicken breast and some rice and vegetables. I haven't had chicken in a while. The last time I tried to eat chicken, the smell made me nauseated. I really hope it doesn't happen now. I take a couple bites of my rice and vegetables. My chicken taunts me, and I feel my stomach turn a little bit.

"Chloe?" I look up at my dad, who has a look of concern written all over his face. "Honey, you're green. Are you feeling okay?"

My eyes begin to fill with tears, yet again. I'm such a mess right now. "I-I'm fine, but there is something I need to tell you guys." I take a deep breath. "I'm pregnant."

Silence fills the room, and neither of them says anything. They're both staring at me with looks that I don't recognize. My hands twist nervously in my lap, and my stomach turns violently, but I swallow it down. I haven't puked yet, and I don't plan on starting now.

"Well, okay. Who is the father?" This comes from my pops.

"I'd rather not say until I tell him, which I plan on doing soon." I'm surprised he seems so calm—I figured if anyone was going to lose it, it'd be him.

"How could you be so irresponsible?" My eyes fly to my dad. I honestly thought he'd be happy or at least take it better than Pops.

"Ian," my pops says with a hand on his arm.

"You're thirty-one years old. Shouldn't you

know better than to let this happen? It's Stacy's nephew, isn't it? For God's sake, he's a fucking kid." I jerk as if he's slapped me.

Pops gets up. "Ian, you need to lay off. We need to talk about this." He comes around until he's next to me and grabs my hand. "When are you due, baby girl?"

"J-January thirtieth." My voice trembles, and my body jerks when I hear a door slam. Tears roll down my face. "He's so mad at me."

"No, baby girl. He's just in shock. You know he's going to love being a grandpa. Just give us time to get used to the idea." He hugs me tight before leaning back and kissing both my cheeks. "I'm going to be a grandpa." I burst into more tears and wrap my arms tight around him.

"I love you, Dad."

I leave shortly after that because I'm tired and Dad still isn't back from wherever he went. Just as long as it was away from me, I guess.

My cats greet me at the door and follow me as I move into the living room. I sit down on my blue, red, and cream checkered chaise lounge. Ragnar and Lagertha jump up and rub against me. "Mommy had a bad night. Your grandpa is mad at me." Again, the stupid tears begin to fall. "I didn't do it on purpose. I think I just need to get a good night's sleep."

I go through my nightly routine and change into my nightgown. As I stare at the ceiling, I plan when and how I'm going to tell Joe, and hopefully it'll go better than when I told my dads.

Chapter Two

Joe

I park my squad car and climb out, making my way toward the red BMW convertible in front of me. She's blatantly watching me as I approach. The closer I get, the more I can see how fucking hot she is. Even though I can tell she's had work done, it doesn't keep my dick from taking notice.

"Hi, officer," she purrs. "Did I do something wrong?"

"Do you know how fast you were going?" She shakes her head. "Ten miles over the speed limit, and I'm going to have to have your license and registration."

She holds them out to me. I grab them and tell her I'll be right back. I feel her eyes on my ass as I head back to my car.

Not to sound cocky, but I know I'm a good-looking guy. I've never had trouble getting the ladies; they've just naturally flocked to me. This traffic stop is no different than any of the others where the chicks have been hot.

I'll admit sometimes they've shown up at the bar a lot of us officers hang out in after a shift, and I may or may not have gone home with them, fucked all night, and then left when it was over. I prefer to keep it casual—I like easy and uncomplicated. My one real relationship was a bonafide disaster, and I'm never going through that again.

When I run her license, I look at it closely. Her eyes are a bright blue, and the more I look at them, the more they remind me of Chloe's. Fuck, I haven't been able to stop thinking about her since our night together. I have one word that describes Chloe in bed: energetic. She gave me a run for my money, and I've never been with someone who can have multiple orgasms the way she did. She's a squirter too, and that was such a turn-on.

Fuck, she was the sweetest pussy I've ever had. One night wasn't nearly enough with her, but she lives four hours away, and I don't know how I'd be received if I just showed up. Hell, I haven't been with anyone since her. It's not like I couldn't find anyone—hell, I've had them throwing themselves at me—but it's the raven-haired beauty who fills my mind.

I write out her ticket and get back out of my car. "Here you go. Next time, slow down." I flash her my signature smile, tip my chin, and then head back to my car.

Back in my squad car, I look at the clock and see it's time to head back to the station. When I reach it, I spot my brother-in-law, Ben, pull in too. "What's up, bro?" I call out as I get out of my car.

"Hey, Joe, how's it going?"

"Good…fuck, it was a long one today." We live in a smaller area, and sometimes it's just not that exciting.

"Agreed. Guess what?" I raise a brow at him. "Abby's pregnant. We weren't really trying, but you know…sometimes things just happen."

I grab him and pull him into a hug, slapping his back. "That's fantastic. I'm thrilled for you guys. Have you told our parents?" My folks love Ben and love how he helped Abby heal after she'd been sexually assaulted. Now she's the adopted mom of Ben's daughter, Natalie, and had two more kids, Dalton and Rion.

"Yeah, they watched the kids for us so we could go out to dinner and celebrate. We told them when we came back. Your mom is insistent that this baby be a girl. I think your sister secretly wants one, and honestly I kind of want one too. I already promised her that I'd get snipped after this one. Four kids are plenty." I've never seen a look of such pure joy on someone's face before.

We head inside to get changed back into our street clothes.

A little later, I pull into the parking lot of my apartment complex and climb out of my truck. It's a small complex with only six units but lots of amenities. There's a gym, a pool, and a rec room. I even pay a little extra to have a garage, which holds my Harley. I park and head up to my apartment and let myself inside.

It's the stereotypical bachelor pad: huge flat screen on the wall, Xbox One console sitting on the floor. An oversized brown sectional fills my living room. The decorations I do have are only there because my mom and sisters insisted that I needed them so they bought me some stuff.

In my bedroom, I change into some basketball shorts and a muscle shirt. I grab my ear buds and iPhone. Outside, I begin jogging at a slow pace, just to warm up. It's when I'm a couple blocks away that I pick up the pace. My feet pound the pavement as the Foo Fighters play in my ears.

My thoughts drift to my sister, and I smile. Words can't even describe how happy I am for them, but I seriously don't know how they do it. Natalie is the oldest, and she's almost eight, Dalton is three, almost four, and Rion is two and a half. My sister never looks tired and is always freaking smiling. She and Ben are the perfect couple. He treats her like a queen, and she treats him like a king.

I reach my complex and head right to the fitness room, thankful it's empty. I lift for an hour before heading back to my apartment and taking a hot shower. The water beats down on me, relaxing my tired muscles.

I close my eyes, and visions of my night with Chloe flood my mind. We had taken a shower mainly to clean off, but her wet, naked body pushed up against mine had shattered my restraint. I had picked her up and fucked her against the wall until she came with a cry. I pulled out, and she had dropped to her knees, sucking me off until I came hard down her throat.

I realize my hand is wrapped around my cock,

and it's hard beneath my hand. I groan as erotic images flit through my mind. I feel my balls draw up tight. A tingle starts at the base of my spine as I imagine my fist is her tight pussy. I come with a grunt and a groan, my come splashing against the shower wall.

After rinsing off, I climb out of the shower, and with a towel wrapped around my waist, I head into the kitchen and grab a beer out of the fridge. I flop down on my couch and turn on ESPN. I'm only half watching.

Lately I feel like I've been in a funk, and I don't know how to get out of it. It feels like life is moving around me at a fast pace, but I seem to be standing still. I can't even say that it's because of Chloe, because honestly, I started feeling that way before we slept together.

I've felt restless, unsettled. My dad seems to think it's because I'm ready for more out of my life—that I'm ready to settle down—but that can't be it, can it? I'm twenty-four years old. I've enjoyed lots of women since I began to take notice of them. I've always loved uncomplicated, and the one time I tried to take it seriously, it went to shit real quickly.

Tracey and I met while I was still at the community college with Violet, taking our pre-requisites. From the start, I should've known it was wrong. We didn't fit; I've always been social and make friends everywhere I go—girls and guys flock to me. But she hated going to bars and kept to herself a lot. She shied away from people she didn't know.

Whenever we went out, I liked to put in extra

effort to look good, but Tracey preferred running shorts, t-shirts, and tank tops more than anything. She never wore makeup, either.

None of that bothered me, though. I thought she was beautiful, and I told her that repeatedly. But it was four months into our relationship when I noticed her mood swings. Sometimes they happened so rapidly that I could barely keep up. I worried about her all of the time. My grades started falling because I was afraid to leave her alone. I'm not sure if I thought she would hurt herself or afraid she'd hurt someone else.

Two months after that, her parents finally told me that Tracey was bipolar and her rapid mood swings were called "rapid cycling." They were in the process of getting her into a treatment center that specialized in bipolar disorder.

We broke up right before she left. It was amicable, but it still fucking hurt. She wrote me for a while after she left, and the last letter I got was a year and a half ago. Tracey said she was doing great and the meds she was on were the right mix to keep her level. At the end of the letter, she threw me for a loop and told me she was getting married, and I honestly felt my heart break a little.

Oh, I'm over it and her now. We weren't meant to be, and I'm okay with that, but maybe that's when a little bit of an unsettled feeling started. I finish my beer and grab another, trying to shake off the melancholy. Something needs to change.

***

I pull up in front of my parents' home. It's my dad and uncle's birthday, and my mom is throwing them a birthday party. My mom has made a big deal out of birthdays for as long as I can remember. It was always breakfast and presents in bed the morning of.

Dad and Uncle Dustin are getting a couple rounds of golf from me. I know they don't always have time to go, but buying them a round is the least I could do. I climb out and make my way up to the front door. I don't bother knocking because it swings open as I reach it.

"Uncle Joey!" Natalie flings herself into my arms. "I've missed you!"

"I've missed you too, baby girl." I step inside, and it's chaos. My cousin Carrington is here with her husband, Damien. He's with the DEA. Their little twins are playing on the floor with my sister's youngest. Abby and Cari are sitting with them on the floor.

"Hey, guys." Abby comes toward me with Rion in her arms. I reach out to stroke his caramel-colored curls, and he reaches for me too. I take him from his mom. I bend down and kiss Abby's cheek. "Congratulations."

She smiles so big I'm surprised her cheeks don't crack. "Ben was supposed to let me tell you, but he's been so excited about it." Abby rubs a hand over her little baby bump. "This is the last one. Four kids are enough, especially since we weren't planning on this one." She points to her belly.

Cari comes over and gives me a kiss and a hug. How she can carry both of those kids without any help is beyond me. I'd probably drop one or both of them. I carry Rion as I follow Natalie through the house and out the back door where the rest of my family is.

Rion sees my mom, immediately squirms to get out of my arms, and runs right to her. I go to my dad and uncles Dustin and Luke, giving them all back-slapping hugs. Ben and Damien join our little huddle. Everyone is here except for Violet and Luke Jr., because they're both in Louisiana for school.

My dad throws his arm around my shoulders. "Thanks for coming. I know you have a busy social calendar, so it's nice to know you haven't forgotten about us." Of course he's being a smart ass, but rightfully so. I've been known to blow off family stuff for a woman. I'm not proud of it, but what can I say? I'm not the smartest sometimes.

"Har har har. Very funny, Dad. I had to come and celebrate you getting old...I mean, older." He puts me in a headlock and acts like he's punching me.

I excuse myself and go to my mom, kissing her cheek. "Hey, Momma." She's got all three grandkids sitting with her and my aunt Stacy. "How's Violet?"

My aunt smiles widely. "She's great. She's pregnant and excited. Diego's over the moon." She looks at my mom. "When did we become old enough to be grandparents?"

Mom flashes her a smile. "I don't know, but I love it, and you will too. Just don't go cray cray like Bellamy."

My aunt Bellamy was over trying to take Cari's

35

twins so much that they finally had to set up scheduled days when she could have the babies. These women are all crazy for their grandkids, but isn't that the way it's supposed to be?

"I'll have to call Vi and congratulate her. Where're Parker and Haddie?"

"Your brother forgot to ask for tonight off, so he's working but should be here by seven or eight, and Haddie ran to the store to get more ice cream."

I hear the sliding glass door open, and I hear a familiar voice that immediately gets my dick hard. "Tay Tay!"

I turn to find Chloe come rushing out to my aunt and uncle. My eyes take in her gorgeous body. She's wearing jean shorts that hug her ass and show off long, lean legs. The faded Mötley Crüe t-shirt hugs her tits and shows off her trim waist. Her raven hair is piled up on top of her head.

She goes to my mom and dad, hugging them both. "Thanks for inviting me. Carter's sorry he couldn't come, but the marching band has a competition this weekend so they're out of town."

I grab beers for all the men because, as always, we gather around the grill while the women are all doing whatever it is that they're doing. I've yet to talk to Chloe, but that doesn't mean that whenever she's around that my eyes don't follow her. Earlier, she and Aunt Stacy were talking off to the side, and it seemed serious, and the nosy part of me wanted to find out what was happening with her.

The only thing I've noticed is that since their talk, my aunt keeps looking in my direction...weird.

"Uncle Joey." I look down and find Natalie

standing next to me.

"What is it, sweetheart?"

"Can you come over and play with us tomorrow?" I try to get over to see my sister's kids as often as I can. Sometimes I work crazy hours, so it's not always possible. I pick up a lot of the slack so Ben can stay on first shift, which he just started working a few months ago. I don't mind it—it's not like I have anyone waiting at home for me.

God, why does that feel depressing all of a sudden?

I kneel in front of the little princess. "Yes, I'll come play with you tomorrow. Maybe you and I can sneak away for some ice cream. How does that sound?"

Natalie throws her arms around my neck. "That sounds great! Did you hear Mommy's got another baby in her belly? I hope it's a girl, because I'm tired of yucky boys."

I throw my head back and laugh. I look around and find my dad and Ben smiling at her and all her cuteness. Chloe comes walking up and looks at us, her eyes going soft, but then it quickly disappears, and she starts backing away. I kiss Natalie and set her down before moving toward Chloe.

"Chloe? Hey, how are you?"

"I'm good. How are you?" I can see the pulse in her neck, and it's pounding rapidly. Does she feel awkward being around me now?

Without thinking, I reach out, tucking a loose strand of hair behind her ear. "I've been good. Been thinking about you a lot." Her eyes widen, and I could get lost in their blue depths. "Why is that so hard to believe? We had a great time, didn't we?"

"Yeah, we did." She looks down at her shoes and then back up at me. "I'm here until tomorrow, but could we talk before I head back home?"

"Is everything okay with you?" I look her over, and she looks fine. I don't see anything wrong with her.

"Oh yeah, I'm fine. I just wanted to talk, but if you're busy, that's cool."

Moving in closer to her, I cage her in with my arms. "How about we go somewhere and talk after the party?"

"Okay, sure."

My fingers rub against her soft cheek, and I watch her pearly white teeth bite into her lower lip. Her cheeks turn a gorgeous pink color.

She scoots out from in between me and the railing and hustles into the house. My dad and uncle are by the grill, and while Uncle Dustin flips burgers, my dad's staring at me with a curious look on his face. I give him a chin lift and then head inside.

After presents, cake, and ice cream, the party is winding down. My baby sister, Haddie, and I pick up the trash so the parental units can sit and relax. Dad's got Mom in her usual spot, on his lap. Abby's sitting next to Ben on the sofa, and Rion is asleep in her lap.

Chloe is sitting next to Aunt Stacy and Cari, who's holding her twins in her arms. The munchkins are passed out. I feel someone come and stand next to me. It's Damien. "The twins are really cute, but man, they're busy," I say. "How do you guys keep up with them?"

"I don't know. To be honest, Cari does a lot, and the girl is Wonder Woman. I feel like she's always on the move with them, and she never complains. She wants to have another baby, but I want to wait until the twins are closer to two."

"Jesus, what if you have twins again?"

"We'll certainly be used to it. I'd do anything to make her happy." He moves farther into the room and sits down on the floor in front of Cari, taking their sleeping son, Ryder, from his wife's arms.

My uncle Luke grabs his granddaughter from Chloe, and she gets up and comes toward me. "I'm going to head back to the inn, but here's my number. If you still want to talk or can talk, just give me a call."

I take the slip of paper and watch her move around the room saying goodbye to everyone. I want to follow her, but it would look a little suspicious if I left with her. Although I *am* an adult, I don't want my family asking questions I don't have answers to.

Uncle Dustin and Aunt Stacy walk her out. I'll stay another half hour, and then I'll make my way to Chloe. Hell, if I knew she was coming, I would've brought my spare set of keys and let her chill at my place. I program her number into my phone and then stick it back in my pocket.

When it's safe for me to go, I say goodbye to everyone and help Abby and Ben load their brood up in their minivan. I promise my mom when I tell her goodbye that I'll come over for dinner one night next week. Even though we're all growing up and moving away, she still insists on family dinners at least once a week.

Of course, with Abby and her brood, it's a chaotic affair, but my mom loves it.

In my truck, I send Chloe a text.

Joe: Hey, it's Joe. Do you still want to talk?

She answers almost immediately.

Chloe: Yeah that'd be great. Do you want to come to me or do you want me to come to you?

So many dirty thoughts come to my mind, and my dick starts getting hard.

Joe: Hmmm…I could take that so many ways. Why don't you come to me?

Chloe: ;)

I text her my address, and I rush home so I can beat her there. Once inside, I run through my place and make sure it's at least a little tidy.

A knock on my door has me moving toward it. I take a deep breath, reach for the doorknob, and pull it open. Chloe gives me a smile.

"Hey." I love the sexy, raspy tone of her voice.

I reach out and grab her hand, pulling her inside my place. With my foot I kick my door shut, and I blindly reach out and lock the door. I can't and don't stop myself from cupping her face in my hands. "Fuck me, you're beautiful."

"You're not so bad yourself." She pushes up on her toes until her lips are a hair's breadth away from mine. "This isn't why I wanted to see you."

My arm slides around her waist, and I pull her tightly to me. Her breasts are pressed firmly against me, and I really wish they were bare right now. I reach up and pull the pins out of her hair until her raven locks come tumbling down around her.

Her breath is minty as it hits my lips in little puffs. "Why did you come?" I whisper against her lips.

"I'm pregnant." She freezes, as do I.

I grab her arms and push her away from me. "What?"

"I'm pregnant. It's yours." I open my mouth to speak, but she holds up her hand. "Before you and after you, there hasn't been anyone, at least not for a long time. It's up to you whether you want to be involved or not, but I'm keeping this baby and am prepared to do it alone."

I can't speak. My mouth opens and closes, but no sound comes out. You don't have as much sex as I have without being extremely careful. My brain is barely functioning right now.

"You should go." With all of my might, I ignore her crestfallen expression. Fuck, I don't know what to say to her right now.

She grabs her purse, and my door's shutting before I know what's happening. My feet come unglued, and I take off running down the stairs to guest parking, but her taillights are the only things I see in the distance.

"Fuck."

Chapter Three

Chloe

Two weeks later

With a steady hand, I use my lucky tweezers to place the cushion-cut sapphire into the unique wedding set that I've been working on for the past couple of days. The groom was awesome to work with because he came in with pictures of what he wanted and was very clear on the design.

Those are my favorite clients because there is no hemming and hawing about ideas. He had a plan, and I'm executing it.

My stomach rolls, and I take a deep breath. I don't know where the constant nausea has suddenly come from, but I have to be so careful about what I eat or drink now. My clothes in just two weeks' time have gotten looser. I've been reduced to eating saltines with a little dab of peanut butter on them.

Pops has been over a lot, making sure I'm okay, and Dad still isn't speaking to me. I've tried texting him and calling him, but he's not answering. Pops says he's been working on him, but I told him I didn't want Dad forced or guilted into talking to me. I'm not going to feel bad about it because I didn't get pregnant on purpose, but I'm not going to regret this innocent baby, either.

I haven't heard from Joe, but considering his reaction, I'm not surprised. A part of me wants to be sad, but another part of me says that it's not worth the effort. Plus I've felt so terrible lately I don't have the energy to care.

I focus back on the rings. The engagement ring is gorgeous with its platinum band and a sapphire surrounded by tiny diamonds as the centerpiece. The wedding band is thin with matching diamonds set into it. With all of the gems, I was worried about them looking like costume jewelry, but instead they look vintage. After polishing them up, I place them on the little stand and grab my phone to take pictures.

When I stand up to grab a jewelry box, I have to grab my chair because I feel like I'm going to fall over. I take some deep breaths and the feeling passes, but my heart feels like it's racing. I grab my herbal tea and take a small sip, and thankfully it stays down. Too bad it tastes like ass, and I'd kill for a nonfat caramel macchiato.

I give the groom a quick call to tell him the rings are ready, and he's so excited he's heading my way now. This is why I love doing what I do. Last year for my dads' thirty-fifth anniversary, I made them matching rings with mine and Carter's birthstones and left enough room to add spouses and children someday, and obviously my child will be the first.

Ten minutes goes by, and I'm sipping my tea when Mr. Harmon sticks his head in the back. "Chloe. Mr. Peterson is here for his rings."

I grab the box. "Do you want to see them first?"

He takes the box from me and slowly opens it. Very carefully, he pulls them out and looks at them. "Chloe, these are gorgeous. Is this a vintage setting?"

"No, sir. But that was the look he was going for."

"Well, I think you're going to have a very satisfied customer." He wipes his fingerprints off and then places them back in the box. I take the box from him and stand up, swaying slightly. Luckily, he doesn't notice.

When I'm in the middle of a design, I tend to dress more for comfort, and Mr. Harmon has never complained. My hair is in a knot on top of my head, and I'm wearing cut-off sweats, another vintage t-shirt, and my Adidas. My shirt and shorts are covered by a smock, though, but crap, I think I forgot to put on makeup today.

My customer is standing on the other side of the counter, and I can tell he's excited. He sees me come through the doors, and his energy is palpable. "Hi, Mr. Peterson. Come have a seat, and I'll show you the set." I take him over to my desk where I usually do my consultations.

We both sit, and I hand him the box. He opens it very slowly and pulls the engagement ring out first. "This is everything I wanted it to be." *Oh no*. My eyes immediately fill with tears. "My Sarah is going to love it." *His Sarah*? Oh wow. This guy wants me to lose it and start crying all over him.

"I'm so pleased you're happy with them. Your Sarah is very lucky." He pays the remaining balance, and I place the box in a decorative gift box with a purple satin bow. I grab a little gift bag from under the counter. My vision goes hazy, and I feel my heartbeat in my ears. I grip the counter but feel my fingers begin to tingle.

"Are you okay? Somebody help!" I hear someone yell, and then arms wrap around me before everything goes dark.

A steady beep pulls me from my sleep. I hear soft talking, and my eyes flutter open. There is a low light shining down on me. My eyes scan the room, and it looks like I'm in the hospital, but why? It comes back to me—feeling dizzy at work, my vision going hazy, and then me falling to the ground.

When I had come to, my boss was hovering over me, and then there were paramedics there. I told them I was pregnant, and they immediately loaded me up onto the gurney. I'd asked Mr. Harmon to call my dads as I was wheeled past him.

I turn my head to the side and see Dad and Pops sitting next to my bed, and Dad's holding my hand. "Hey," I say softly. They both get up, and my dad begins to cry, hugging me tightly to him. He takes a deep breath and gets control of himself.

"You sure scared us, baby girl."

"I know, I'm sorry. I haven't been feeling good lately, and I've been too nauseous to eat much. I've been living on saltines and peanut butter and herbal tea. I should've called my doctor, especially when I felt my shorts getting looser." He strokes my hair out of my face. "I'm sorry, Daddy. Don't be mad at me anymore."

"Oh sweetheart, you don't have any reason to apologize. I'm the one who's sorry." He kisses my forehead before moving so Pops can get to me.

"The doctor popped in a few minutes ago, but he let you sleep. I'll go get him." My pops disappears, and my dad grabs my hand.

"Did you guys call Carter?" I know my brother is probably freaking out.

"Yeah, he should be here anytime. Honey, he said he was calling Joe." My eyes widen. "He wasn't planning on telling us that it's Joe's baby until you were ready, even though we figured it out. He was going to call Joe and tell him about you."

"Daddy, he doesn't want this baby. I wish you guys would've waited before you called him. If he shows up, it'll be out of guilt, and I don't want that."

"Shit, I'm sorry. We didn't even think about that. We are just screwing this all up. Maybe I'll call Stacy and have her run interference."

I nod my head because that sounds like a great idea, and I tell my dad that. He excuses himself to make the call when my pops comes back in followed by a man in a lab coat. "Chloe, this is Dr. Swanson."

"Hi, Chloe. Can you tell me about your symptoms and when they started?"

He helps me raise the head of the bed. I want to be sitting up. "Certain things have made me a little queasy, like chicken, but not constantly. The constant nausea started around two weeks ago and has progressively gotten worse. The only food I've been able to tolerate is peanut butter and crackers. Even then I can only tolerate a couple bites."

"We're going to prescribe something for you for the nausea, but I want you to try taking some ginger and thiamine first. I'll write out how much to take and when. If those pills don't work, then you'll need to start Zofran. If it gets any worse with the meds, you'll need to follow up with your doctor because you may need IV fluids, but I do want you following up with her anyway." He scribbles some things down and then looks back up at me. "Your IV's about empty—I'll get your discharge papers and send the nurse to unhook you and let you go home. I want you to take the next couple of days easy, and let's hope the ginger and thiamine work. You take care."

He takes his leave, and I sit up more in bed and swing my legs over the side. My pops sits down next to me. "I think you should come home with us. Let us take care of you."

"Dad, no, I'm seriously okay. I don't need to be disrupting your lives. I'll be fine. You guys live five minutes from my house, so I can always call you if I need you. Plus, who would take care of my babies?" Sure, they've watched my cats before, but they don't give them cuddles like I do.

"Fine, but after we get you settled at home, your dad and I will get your medicine for you. We'll also get your car from the jewelry store," Pops says before moving out of the way so the nurse can unhook my IV and give me my discharge papers and prescriptions.

Dad insists on carrying me out of the hospital while Pops gets their SUV and pulls it up in front of the doors. Pops shakes his head at Dad. "Ian, her legs aren't broken. She can walk."

He just rolls his eyes. "I know, but our baby is sick, and I don't want her walking, so just let me do it."

Dad sits me in the front seat and buckles me in. "Daddy, I can do it myself."

"I know, but I have to make up for being a complete dick. My baby's having a baby. I'm going to be his or her favorite." He gives Pops a look.

I hear Pops whisper something under his breath about being the favorite. "Seriously?" I say. "You do realize you'll be my child's only grandparents, right? You can share the duties of being the favorites."

They both get quiet, and I choose to ignore it. I know why, too—it's because they probably think I should let Joe's parents know so that they can decide to be involved with their grandchild or not, but what if it's not my place to tell them? What if they hate me? What if Tay Tay and Dustin hate me and take Joe's side and then I lose them?

We pull up in front of my house, and I see Carter's Jeep is in the driveway. Before I can get out of the SUV, my dad already has the door open and is trying to pick me up, but I manage to shoo him away. "Daddy, I'm fine. Seriously...please let me walk."

As soon as my feet touch the ground, they both

have an arm around me. It's overkill, but I'll let it go for now. The front door opens, and my brother is standing there. "Always trying to be the center of attention, huh?"

Ragnar and Lagertha both move in front of Carter and greet me with matching meows. "Hi, my precious babies. Mommy is okay."

"Oh, brother," I hear Dad groan from behind me, but as soon as they step in behind me, they both curse. That's when I realize someone is standing in the middle of my living room.

"Joe? What are you doing here?"

He walks toward me hesitantly. "Your brother got ahold of me and told me you were sick. I wanted to come check on you myself."

I give my brother a look that I hope conveys that I'm not too happy with him. Pops gets in front of me, but I try to move back in front. "Boy, you've got a lot of nerve showing up here. I know you told her to leave when she told you about the baby."

"Dad, that's enough. Please let us talk, okay? Can you guys go get my prescriptions filled? You also said you'd get my car. I'll be fine, and we're just going to talk." Finally, I get them to go and turn back around to face Joe.

God, why does he have to look good? He's wearing a t-shirt that is molded to his lean, muscular frame and jeans that cling to his firm thighs. A baseball cap sits on his head, creating a shadow over his blue eyes.

"Thanks for coming, and as you can see, I'm okay." I walk into the kitchen and fill up my kettle with water before setting it on the stove. My eyes stay on it even when I feel Joe enter the room. His presence is so much larger than life that he fills any room that he enters.

I continue to ignore him while I wait for the water to boil. "Listen, I know I hurt you, and I'm sorry. You just caught me by surprise, and I didn't know what to do or say." I stay facing the stove, and I hear him sigh. "I want to be involved in our child's life. I want to know him or her."

"Okay, thanks. I'll keep you posted."

"You'll keep me posted? Well, gee, thanks." He sounds pissed, and of course I feel bad.

"What else do you want me to say, Joe? Your first reaction was to tell me to leave." My stomach picks this moment to rebel against me and this time violently. I make it to the sink just in time, but because I've barely eaten, it's mostly bile. I dry heave a few times and feel Joe's hand on my back, gently rubbing it.

The tea kettle whistles, and I stand up to go to it, but Joe stops me. "I'll take care of that." He moves away, and I turn my head to see him shut my stove off and move the kettle.

Joe moves back toward me and scoops me up in his arms. "What are you doing?"

"You need to rest. Which bedroom is yours?" We reach my room, and my cats are both lounging on my bed. "What kind of cats are those? They're fucking huge."

I can't help but laugh. "That's Ragnar and Lagertha. They're Maine Coons. They're named after my favorite characters from the show *Vikings*."

Joe lays me down on top of my bed, and

immediately both my babies snuggle into me. He just shakes his head and leaves my room. Is he leaving? Wow, not even a goodbye. Of course, he returns a few minutes later with a cup in his hand.

"I didn't know what you wanted in your tea, so I left it plain." I sit up in bed and take the mug from him.

"Thanks. I hate tea, so it doesn't really matter what I do to it because it all tastes like a dirty dishrag." Joe throws his head back and laughs. It's a rich, full-bodied sound that creates little flutters in my stomach. He looks back down at me, and the smile on his face is so beautiful it takes my breath away.

"I've never heard it described that way before."

We lapse into an awkward silence. I set my mug down and pick up Laggie. "Sweet baby kitty." She answers me with a meow. The bed compresses next to me as Joe sits down so close to me we're practically touching.

Joe grabs Lagertha from my lap and holds her up so she's facing him. "Which one is this?"

"Lagertha." I'm waiting for him to make fun of me.

"Are you a shield maiden?" he asks. Her answer is another meow, and she doesn't look happy. Ragnar doesn't like being ignored, so he puts his paws on Joe's upper back and begins to purr loudly. "These are the coolest fucking cats I've ever seen. The one behind me is Ragnar?"

"Yes, and thank you, they are pretty cool." I grab my tea, taking a small sip when I hear the front door open. I expect it to be the dads and Carter but smile

51

widely when Eli walks into my bedroom. Eli is half-black and half-Mexican and has bleached hair dyed dark blue. His dark chocolate eyes take in Joe sitting next to me on the bed and then look to me.

"Hi, honey." I climb off the bed and gingerly walk toward him. "Did Carter call you?"

"Yeah, he said you fainted. Is this him?" He looks to Joe.

"Joe, this is Eli, my best friend, bandmate, and pain in my ass. Eli, this is Joe Carmichael. He's Vi's cousin and well…um…you know." They shake hands, and I can tell Eli wants to try and intimidate him, but Joe's got at least two inches and a hell of a lot more muscle on him.

"Nice meeting you, Eli."

"You too." Eli looks at me and mouths *fucking hot.*

I shake my head and roll my eyes as I hear Joe chuckle. Joe knows he's hot—I don't know why I should've even been surprised that Eli had that reaction.

My parents and brother return shortly after, and honestly, I want everyone gone. I'm grateful they want to help and take care of me, but they'll hover, and I don't want or need anyone hovering over me.

I'm not sure why Joe's still here, but he is and hasn't really left my side. Both of my dads keep giving him dirty looks, but Joe takes it in stride. He even tries to engage them in conversation. Eli has his arm wrapped around me, and his lips are tipped up in a smile.

"This is positively the most entertaining show I've seen in a long time."

A giggle escapes before I can stop it. "I know, right?" I kiss Eli's cheek before moving toward my family. "I love you guys, but you can go now. You all have to work, and I'm obviously going to stay home tomorrow."

Carter looks at Joe, then back at me. "Are you sure?"

"Thank you, but yes, I'm sure. I already feel bad that you got pulled away from work." I turn to look at my fathers. "I'll be fine. I've got my medicine, and you're close by in case I need you."

"Fine, but you call us before you go to bed," Pops says as he kisses my forehead.

Next is Dad, who hugs me tight. "I love you, baby girl." He punctuates his words with a kiss to my cheek.

"Eli, let's go. You need to get home, too. I don't need you going all mother hen on me too." I turn to Joe. "I'll be right back unless you're planning on leaving too."

"I'll wait right here." I nod and follow my family outside and watch them all drive away.

Nervous anticipation fills me as I enter my house and find Joe where I left him, in the kitchen. I lean against the doorjamb and watch him. He's slathering saltines with peanut butter and arranging them on a plate. "I can't eat all of those."

"They're actually for both of us. Your brother said this is the only thing you've been able to eat. If I can't take you to dinner, then this is the next best thing." Grabbing the plate, he leads me to the kitchen table. After setting the plate down, he pulls my chair out.

"Thank you for this." We silently munch on the peanut butter crackers. The salty and sweet mixture tastes delicious, but I really wish I could eat something else. My cats sit on the floor in between us. Ragnar is hoping for a spare crumb, and Lagertha just loves being where her brother is.

Joe finishes off the crackers and puts the dirty plate in my sink. He moves through my kitchen with ease, making me another cup of tea.

"How involved do you plan on being? How is this going to work with you four hours away?"

He sits across from me, and I take a sip of my tea, waiting for him to answer. "I'd like to be involved as much as you'll let me. The distance might make it hard, but I can come up whenever I have time off."

"Why would you want to spend that much time here?"

He raises his eyebrow. "Why wouldn't I? Chloe, you're the mother of my child. Shouldn't we get to know each other better?"

That makes sense. We're going to be raising a child together to some capacity. It's only logical that we get to know each other. "You're right. Sorry, this is just all crazy, and it wasn't planned. I'm a planner. Things have to be a certain way. I don't deal with change well, which isn't good because kids are unpredictable. Hell, this pregnancy has been unpredictable already." I lay my head down on the table. "I'm going to be a terrible mother."

Tears threaten to fall…again, but I push them back. I've never been a crier, but this baby is turning me into a freaking crybaby. I only have vague recollections of my mom, and honestly I don't know if they're good or bad. It's just random images. Carter was too young to remember her at all. I do remember how I felt the day I met Ian and Garrett: Dad and Pops. I felt safe and immediately loved.

Not just by them, but the whole family as well. I thought I'd drown in all the love they gave us. Tay Tay became my favorite person the moment I met her. She always looked like a Disney princess to me. Whenever we'd go down to visit Uncle Gary and Aunt Renée, I'd always stay with my Tay Tay.

Images assault me of a night I wish I'd forget. Stacy had been involved with a DEA agent. When she found out he was married, she broke it off, but he wouldn't take no for an answer. I'd been sleeping over at her house when I got up to go to the bathroom. A man covered in tattoos stood in the hallway asking me about her and Dustin.

He'd told me if I told anyone, he'd hurt my Tay Tay. It took a long time to get over that and to not freak out when Stacy wasn't around. It caused a rift between her and Pops, but they eventually made up...I haven't thought about that night in a long time. Why now?

"Are you okay?" I look at Joe, who is looking at me with concern written on his face.

"Yeah, sorry. My mind just wandered off."

He grabs my hand. "Are you sure? You look troubled."

"The baby has my hormones going bonkers, and it's just got me thinking about my birth mom or what I can remember. That isn't much, but she obviously was a horrible mother. Carter was born and had cocaine in his system; it's why they took us." I swipe angrily at the tears that fall. "What if this baby makes something snap in my brain and I become her?"

The scraping sound of a chair moving has me looking up as Joe gets down on his knees next to me. "No tears, babe. I don't think it happens that way. Everything you're feeling is normal. When my sister was pregnant with Rion, she cried all the time. It was always about little stuff, but to her, it was monumental. It stopped when she got through the beginning. I didn't know your mom, but from what I know of you, I don't think you're the type to do anything that would hurt your child, our child."

I blow out a breath. Joe's so close that his woodsy scent permeates my senses. My breasts tingle, and I feel myself get wet. What is happening to me? I'm like a big jumbled emotional rollercoaster.

Before I can stop myself, I reach out and cup Joe's face. His sky blue eyes bore into me, and I'm lost. Leaning forward, I place my lips against his. They're full but masculine. He immediately takes control of the kiss but keeps it soft. His hand moves under my shirt. He reaches my overly sensitive breasts, and I moan against his mouth.

The sound of a phone ringing breaks the spell, and we break apart. "Shit." Joe looks at his phone and then back at me. "I have to take this." I nod.

"Hey, Mom. Yeah, I'll be there." There's a pause, and he looks at me. "I'm in Atlanta." There's another pause. "I'm visiting Chloe."

I'm shocked he just told her that. I raise an eyebrow, and he just smiles at me. I mouth, *Are you staying?*

He mouths back, *Am I?*

I nod and stand up while Joe talks to his mom, and when I go to move past him, he wraps an arm around my waist and pulls me to stand between his legs. He props his phone up on his shoulder and places his large hand on my lower stomach. I bite my lip as my whole body trembles. He can feel it—I know he can, because his eyes darken.

"Yeah, I'm staying up here tonight. I'll be home tomorrow." A pause. "I will. I love you too." He removes his hand from my stomach and then grabs his phone, disconnecting the call. Joe grips my hips and pulls me to stand further between his legs.

I melt when again he places his large hand on my stomach. "I can't believe a part of me is right inside here," he says reverently.

I pull the ball cap off his head, running my fingers through his dark brown hair. It's shaved close on the sides and around the back and longer on top. I kiss the top of his head but quickly pull away. *What the hell am I doing?*

"Should we get married?"

I freeze. "W-What?"

He looks up at me. "Do you think we should get married? For the baby?"

"No. God, no. We barely know each other. You don't have to marry me to be involved with our baby. It'll be a little difficult at first since you're four hours away, but maybe we can come stay with you on weekends or whenever you'd want to see them. No matter what, I'd never keep your child from you. I'm not that person. My child will not be some pawn used to hurt you or trap you."

Joe smiles a big goofy smile at me. "And you were worried you'd be a bad mom. That right there. What you just said shows the kind of mom you're going to be."

My hands rest on Joe's shoulders. God, he feels firm, and his hands feel so good on me. He's making me confused and super horny, but my stomach is turning. Reluctantly, I pull away. "My stomach is a little iffy right now."

Joe stands up, and before I can protest, he's got me in his arms. I'm finding that he really likes carrying me around. We move into my living room, and he lays me down in the corner of my sectional. It's a loveseat with an attached chaise lounge. The fabric is a soft enduro-suede and a beautiful bluish-gray color.

"I'm getting your pills. Sit tight."

I hear him bang around in my kitchen when both of my cats come strutting in and jump up, settling in next to me. My fingers sift through Ragnar's then Lagertha's soft hair. Their purrs make me smile. I lie down, hugging one of my pillows to my chest. My stomach turns, and I want to die right now...Not really, but this constant nausea is becoming irritating.

Chapter Four

Joe

I pull into my parents' driveway. Before I get out, I take a deep breath. I've been mentally preparing myself to tell my parents about Chloe and the baby.

The more I've had time to think about it, the more I'm fucking excited. Sure, I might be what others assume as being too young, but I want this. I have a feeling the more I get to know Chloe, the more I'm going to want her too.

Last night after getting her pills for her, we watched a movie, but to be honest I barely paid attention to it since she had fallen asleep with her head in my lap. While I watched the movie, my hand sifted through her hair. Her cat Lagertha was curled up in front of her, and Ragnar sat next to me staring at me like a creeper.

After the movie ended, I gently woke her and helped her up. She used the bathroom first and then grabbed me an extra toothbrush. When I stepped out of the bathroom, I wasn't sure if I should lie down on the sofa or go into her room. I didn't want to assume anything.

"Joe? You can sleep in here." Well, that answered that question.

The scent of peppermint hit me as soon as I stepped into her bedroom. That's when I noticed a little machine next to her side of the bed with steam or smoke coming out of it. If memory served, peppermint was good for nausea. I stripped out of my t-shirt and jeans so I was in nothing but my boxer briefs.

Chloe held the blankets up as I slipped in next to her. I wrapped my arm around her waist and pulled her toward me until only an inch separated us. "Is this okay?" My lips ghosted over her forehead.

She snuggled closer to me and wrapped her arm around my waist. "It's great." Chloe's voice sounded sleepy.

In seconds, her soft snores filled the room. I felt the cats both jump onto the bed, curling up at the end. The bed was so comfortable, like sleeping on a firm cloud, and almost big enough for my frame. In just a few minutes, I was out.

My eyes opened, and I felt pressure on my chest. I looked down and smiled. Chloe's head was resting on my chest, her arm wrapped around my waist and our legs tangled. Both of my arms were wrapped around her, holding her tight. I've never been a snuggler, but I could've cuddled her forever…wait, what? Forever is a long time, and I'm not quite sure what our future holds.

Carefully, I slipped out of bed and stealthily

moved around to her side. I grabbed and looked at each bottle until I found peppermint. After reading the bottle, I poured water and four drops of the oil into the little diffuser and turned it on. I stood over the steam and tried to shoo it in her direction.

The cats both looked at me while I threw my pants on but then laid their heads right back down. In the kitchen, I got the water going for her tea and made myself a cup of coffee. I also made some peanut butter and saltines.

When I stepped back into her bedroom, I found her running her fingers through Lagertha's fur. She wore a dreamy smile on her face.

"How are you feeling?" I asked as I set the tray down and handed her the cup of tea. A laugh escaped as I watched her take a sip and then make that adorable, disgusted face.

"I'm not sure yet. Once I'm up and moving, I'll let you know. Thank you for starting my diffuser. I'm hoping the peppermint will help. Can I have a cracker?" I climbed onto the bed and settled in next to her. Grabbing a cracker, I held it up to her lips. She looked at me with a question in her eyes.

"Take a bite." Her eyes went to me and then back to the cracker before she leaned in and bit a small piece off. I watched her plump lips as she chewed the cracker and then swallowed it down.

My dick was hard as a rock, but there was nothing that could be done about it or that I was *going* to do about it. She'd been sick—sick enough to end up in the hospital. It wasn't the time to fuck.

I popped a couple of crackers into my mouth and washed them down with a sip of coffee. Chloe climbed out of bed and slowly made it around to the door to the hallway. I climbed out of bed and followed after her. Standing just outside the door as she went to the bathroom, I listened to make sure she didn't need me.

The toilet flushed, the faucet turned on and off, and the door opened. "I feel okay. I'm a little queasy but not nearly as bad."

"Good. Now let's go get your pills."

Back in the kitchen, I handed her the ginger and thiamine pills and watched her swallow them down.

"Your color is better this morning." I reached out, stroking her cheek. "I'm going to have to get going soon." Moving toward her, I wrapped an arm around her waist. "We're going to talk this week. I want to know how you're doing, and I want the chance to get to know you better."

"Sure thing, bossy." She placed her hands on my chest. "Thank you for coming here. Thank you for showing up and wanting to be a part of our baby's life. I would like for us to get to know each other better, too."

That made me happy, and I couldn't help but smile. "I'll talk to you later."

"Call or text me when you get home." I don't know why, but her saying that created warmth in my chest.

When I went to leave, Chloe walked me to the door. I only meant to hug her, but I ended up picking her up and putting her back against the wall as we kissed. It was just as hot as every other kiss we've shared.

There is no denying that we have great chemistry

physically. It's the mental and emotional stuff that we have to figure out.

Pulling my lips reluctantly away from hers, I took a deep breath. "You make it very hard to think. You're hell on my willpower." She reached between us and palmed my aching cock. "You're torturing me, baby."

That's when Chloe's face paled, then turned green. I quickly carried her into the bathroom, but nothing happened. She gagged a couple of times, but that was it.

"Fuck, I can't leave you like this." My mom would understand.

"Joe, I'm okay. You've got a four-hour drive ahead of you. My parents live super close, as do my brother and Eli. I'm covered. Go be with your family."

"Okay, but you call them right away if you need them. You shouldn't be alone." It didn't sit well with me that she could be getting sick all by herself.

She rested her cheek against my chest, tucked in the spot right under my chin. My arms wrapped around her, and neither one of us spoke.

"I really have to go, but we'll talk later." I kissed her forehead because it was safer for both of us right then.

As I pulled out of Chloe's driveway, she gave me a small wave. I don't know what it was, but I could feel it in my soul that it was going to be hard staying away from her.

Now at my parents, I psych myself up for the news I'm about to give them. Since they're expecting me, I don't bother knocking—I just step inside. I find my dad and baby sister Haddie sitting in the living room. "Hey, guys."

My sister has grown into a beautiful young woman. Her strawberry blonde hair is long with curls that frame her face. She's got pale blue eyes like our mom. Haddie comes to me, wrapping me in a tight hug.

"Hey, big brother."

I kiss her cheek. "What's up, squirt?"

She leads me farther into the room. "Nothing. I start nursing school next month. I'm so excited." Haddie will make a great nurse—she's compassionate and caring. She's always over at Abby and Ben's helping with the kids, especially when Ben works doubles.

"You're going to do amazing." I reach my dad. He stands up to give me a hug. "How are you, old man?"

"Who are you calling old? I could still kick your ass." I follow him into the kitchen, where my mom is leaning against the counter with her Kindle in her hand. She's always been a reader, and she's a multitasking reader too. She'll be reading while vacuuming, dusting, cooking…etc.

All of us kids inherited her love of reading. I read a lot of sports biographies and a few murder mysteries. "Jesus, woman. Do you shower with that thing, too?" My mom looks up and smiles. I love the little gap she has between her front teeth. Haddie's got the same one. It matches their characters completely.

"Hi, honey." She gives me a hug, and I look down at her and smile. I'm still not sure how this tiny woman gave birth to me—I was almost a ten-pound baby—but she did and then had two more after me. Abby isn't my biological sister, but Mom's raised her since she was three.

"Hey, Mom." I bend down and kiss her cheek. "What's for dinner? It smells delicious."

"Turkey Tetrazzini, your favorite. Do you wanna set the table for me?" she asks as she pulls down plates.

I move her out of the way, finishing grabbing everything and taking it to the table. "Is Parker going to be here?" He just started an electrician apprenticeship last year. It's in Charleston, so he's staying with our uncle Cash and Aunt Tessa and their kids during the week.

"No, he's helping your uncle on some big project that they're doing around the house," my dad says as he takes the dish from me. "Your mom and I are really proud of you kids. You're all doing so great."

My stomach dips, and I rub my neck. I hate the idea of disappointing my parents. I know I've caused them some grief for as long as I can remember, but this is far more...I wouldn't say worse, but it's more monumental. This isn't going to just change my life but Chloe's, too.

We finish eating, and Haddie excuses herself to go to a movie with Daisy. As soon as she's gone, I help my dad clean up after dinner.

"What's got you troubled?" My dad leans against the counter, looking at me pointedly.

I swallow the lump in my throat. "You may want to sit down. Mom, can you come in here, please?"

She steps into the kitchen and looks between us.

"What's going on? Are you okay?" Rushing toward me, she cups my face and turns it back and forth. "Are you sick?"

She's such a worrier. "No, it's nothing like that. Please just sit with Dad."

Pacing back and forth in front of them, I try desperately to muster up the courage to say what I have to. I take a deep breath and blow it out slowly. "The night of Vi's wedding, I...I slept with Chloe." It's just like ripping off a Band-Aid. I just need to do it quickly. "She's pregnant, and it's mine. We're going to get to know each other better, and I want to help her raise our child."

Neither of them speaks. They both stare at me, and I can't read either of their expressions. This is worse than the time my mom found the condoms in my room when I was fifteen.

"Please say something," I plead.

My mom is the first one to speak. "How did this happen, Joseph?" *Oh shit,* she's pulling out the full name. "Sweetheart, I love you very much, but you should know better."

"Mom, I swear we were safe. I don't know how it happened." God, that sounds so lame. I've always been safe—even with Tracey, we always used condoms. I'd never wanted to take the chance that birth control pills could fail.

"Son, are you sure it's your baby?" I open my mouth to speak, but my dad holds up his hand. "I really like Chloe, I do, but how can you be sure it's yours?"

That makes me mad because I trust her. Yeah, we don't know each other well, but she doesn't seem like the type to pull any shit like that. "Because I trust her when she says that it's mine. Chloe told me I could be involved as much as I want."

"She lives four hours away. How is it going to work?" This comes from my mom.

"I don't know. We haven't gotten that far. She was in the emergency room yesterday and hasn't been feeling well."

My mom stands up and moves toward me. "What happened? Are her and the baby okay?"

"Yeah, she's just got really bad nausea and has been living off peanut butter and saltines…it caught up with her because she passed out at work. They gave her fluids, and now she's taking ginger pills and has peppermint oil going in a diffuser." I don't like that she's alone. Sure, her parents and brother live close, but they don't live with her.

"That poor thing. I remember what that was like. I was so sick with Parker." She cups my cheek. "In all seriousness, you can't say you're going to be all in and then bail on her. I'm not thrilled that this has happened, but babies are a blessing. You don't necessarily have to be together, but raising a child is a partnership. You two are bound together forever now."

Forever? Why does the thought of forever make me queasy all of a sudden? I'm going to be someone's father.

"Joe?"

I back away from my mom, looking between her and my dad. "I've got to get out of here." Bolting for the door, I can hear my dad calling after me, but

I don't stop. I climb in my car and back out quickly.

After driving around aimlessly, I stop along the river. This spot is where Violet and I would come when either of us needed to talk. God, I wish Vi was here now. I could call her, I guess, but she's basking in newly wedded bliss with Diego. Our kids will be close in age just like we are.

I don't know if I can do this—raise a baby together as some sort of partnership, or raise a baby at all. Sure, I love my niece and nephews, but the best part about them is that they'll go home to their mom and dad.

Chloe's seven years older than I am, but the age thing doesn't bother me. So she's older than I am…big fucking deal, because she doesn't look it, and even if she did, I wouldn't care. She's beautiful and sweet and obviously loved by her family. Plus she's related to my aunt Stacy on her side of the family, and she rocks.

But can I really raise a child with her? Will it work?

The streetlights are on when I finally make it home. Both of my parents have tried calling me, but I've been ignoring them. Inside my apartment, I grab a beer out of the fridge. The hiss of the cap being twisted fills my little kitchen. I toss it in the sink and drink down half of the bottle before pulling it away from my lips.

I pull out my phone, thumb through the contacts, and stop on Chloe's name. I want to take the easy way out and just text her, but I can't do it. She deserves to at least hear the words from my mouth.

Shit. It goes right to voicemail. "This is Chloe—

you know what to do."

After the beep, I take a deep breath. "Hey, Chloe, it's Joe. Listen, I don't want to do this on your voicemail, but I just need to get it out. I don't think I can do this. I'm not ready to be someone's father. I'm so sorry." I disconnect the call. Slamming the rest of my beer down, I grab another and crack it open. I drink this one a little slower, and no matter what, it doesn't make me feel any better about what I just did.

My phone pings, and I see it's a text from Chloe.

Chloe: Ok. I will tell you this one time and one time only. There will be no changing your mind down the road. You don't want to be a father then fine you won't be. When the child's born I'll have papers drawn up so you can sign over all of your rights. Have a good life, Joe.

I read it over and over, and the sinking feeling in my stomach hurts like a son of a bitch. With a flick of my wrist, my phone hits the tiled backsplash in my kitchen. The screen shatters and hits the counter.

"What did I just do?"

Chapter Five

Chloe

It's been three weeks since Joe left me that voicemail. So many times I've wanted to text him, but instead I listen to his message over and over to remind myself I'm doing this alone. My parents have been nosy trying to ask what's going on, but subtly. I've blown them off. I just don't want to deal with telling them that my child's father rejected him or her.

Plus Pops would tell Tay Tay, who would tell Dustin, and then they could say something to Joe, and that's the last thing that I'd want. I do not want Joe guilted into being involved. I had hoped that his voicemail was just his nerves talking, but it clearly wasn't.

The past two weeks I've finally felt good. I'm able to eat some stuff, but my stomach still hates chicken. I'm starting to get a little pooch, and I love it. Of course if I lie on my back it disappears, but I know it's there. I even had to buy bigger bras, and that makes me so happy. My breasts were decent before, and now they're fuller.

It's my dad's birthday today, so I'm going over to my uncle Tom and Aunt Mara's place for his party. My family finally all knows about the baby, and everyone seems to be excited for me. My grandma is ecstatic about being a great-grandma. I think everyone is just excited to have something to look forward to, especially after my uncle Gary passed.

After my shower, I slip into my hot pink maxi sundress. It's hot and humid today, so I put my hair into a twisty bun. I spritz a little sunflower-scented body spray on. My cats follow me into the kitchen, where I grab my purse and keys, and I give each of them a treat.

They both answer with a meow. "I'll be home in a little bit." I look at the calendar as I walk out of the kitchen and pause. I'm almost into the twelfth week of my pregnancy.

I feel like this baby is a girl. I don't know what it is, but I just have this feeling. In my head, I'm already designing her wardrobe. Smiling, I place my hand on my little bump, and then I head out to the car.

As soon as I park down the street from my aunt and uncle's, I climb out of my car. Uncle Tom and Aunt Mara's grandson—my cousin Gabe's youngest boy—comes running down the sidewalk toward me.

"Chloe!"

"Heya, Hunter." He wraps his arms around me. I stroke a hand over his dark blond locks. "Am I the last to arrive?"

"Yep, let's go because I'm starving. Uncle Garrett says you're always late."

I can't deny it because it's totally true. Hand in hand, we make our way down to the house, and there are people everywhere. I love our large, loud family, and our parties usually end in a jam session. My uncle's neighbors are cool, though, and usually come join in and party with us.

Hunter leads me into the backyard, and I run over to my dad. "Happy birthday, Daddy." He hugs me tight and kisses my temple.

"How's my beautiful girl?" He's been hovering since I passed out. I don't know why he's doing it, but my guess is he still feels guilty for how he reacted when he found out I was pregnant.

"I'm good." I hold up the gift bag in my hand. "Open your present."

He knows whatever I get him is usually something I made myself, and we're both criers. He pulls out the jewelry box and looks at me. "Did you make this?" I nod.

When he opens the lid ever so slowly, I don't miss his swift intake of breath. His fingers go to the platinum, diamond-cut box chain around his neck. Inside the box are two round pendants connected by a loop that says, ***I'm so special I have two grandpas to love.*** "Oh, honey. I love it so much." He hands me the box and undoes his chain. I carefully pull the pendant out and slip it onto his chain.

I clasp it for him and finger the round discs. My eyes meet his, and I can see his are glistening, which makes mine glisten too.

"Pops, they're over here." I turn to see Carter come toward us, followed by Pops.

I kiss my brother's cheek before going to Pops, hugging him tight. He lets me go and goes over to Dad, wrapping his arm around his waist. "Look what our talented daughter made for me."

"This is gorgeous, baby girl. I don't wear a chain like your dad, but I might consider it if you made one of these for me, too. Maybe instead of a chain you could do hemp."

I can't believe he wants me to make him one, too. My pops wears a wedding ring—that's it. "Yeah, sure. I'll see what I have at home."

I excuse myself and greet my family. Everyone asks how I'm feeling and if I'm going to find out what I'm having, which I think I am. I want to be ready. Stepping into the house, I spot two familiar faces: Tay Tay and her mom, my aunt Renée, are in the living room.

"Tay Tay!" I run toward her, hugging her tight and then moving toward her mom to hug her. "I've missed you." Aunt Renée kisses both of my cheeks.

My eyes begin to burn when she puts her hand over my little pooch. "Your uncle would be so thrilled for you." Her voice cracks a little.

I place my hand over hers. "Thank you for saying that." I turn to look at Tay Tay. We haven't really talked since everyone found out. Joe is her nephew, which puts her in a weird position. "Please don't be mad at me."

She grabs me and pulls me into a hug. "Honey, I could never be mad at you. I'm sorry about Joe. We were all hoping he'd come around."

I can't answer her right away because I'm afraid I may start to cry. "Who can blame him? He's twenty-four; he should be out sleeping around and enjoying being single. Not strapped to a thirty-one year old. Enough about that. How're Vi and Diego?"

"They're doing great. Vi's having a little girl, and Dustin's so excited about it. He can't wait to be a grandpa. Garrett and Ian both seem excited about you having a baby."

"Yeah, Dad was a little upset at first, but after I got sick, he quickly got over it. Check out the pendant he's wearing. I made it. I can make one similar for Dustin if you think he'd like it." She squeezes my hand and then goes searching for my dads.

After everyone's done eating, we do the birthday cake and then the rest of the presents. The uncles, cousins, and my brother are all setting up to play in the little cul-de-sac. Neighbors start bringing their chairs out, and kids are running around. Next year my child will be here, probably being passed around and loved.

When everyone's set up, I move toward the microphone. Pops comes toward me carrying his guitar. "We'll start with your dad's favorite song."

I give him a smile and turn toward the growing crowd. "Hey y'all, thank you for coming to spend time with us and helping to celebrate my dad's birthday. Daddy, we love you." He blows us a kiss from where he sits with my grandma.

The beginning notes of "One of These Nights"

by the Eagles begin to flow through the speakers, and I begin to sing. Singing has always come naturally to me. I've performed since I was a little girl. Telling a story through song is a gift that I have treasured.

As the night progresses, song after song is played. Everyone's having a good time. Dad's drunker than a skunk and hugging everyone repeatedly. I go into the house to use the bathroom because my stomach feels achy all of a sudden, and when I wipe there's bright red blood on the toilet paper. My heart starts to race when I stand up to see blood in the toilet.

A stabbing pain hits me, and I double over, crying out. *Oh God, my baby.* I'm losing it, I just know it. I stumble out into the hall, and Aunt Mara comes rushing toward me. "Honey, what is it?"

"I-I think I'm losing the baby." I start to sob as I'm hit with another sharp pain and feel a gush rushing down my leg.

Next thing I know, I'm in a flurry of activity. I'm in my pop's arms, and they're loading me into someone's van. Tears pour down my face, someone strokes my hair, and someone is holding my hand.

At the hospital, my brother carries me inside, and they rush me right back. My dad answers all of the questions because I can't stop crying. I feel another warm gush, but this time it feels different. Down in my soul, I know my baby just came out of me, and I begin to sob hysterically.

The nurses move my pops and brother out of the room against their will. I hear Tay Tay tell them she'll stay and take care of me, and she does, holding my hand. When the nurse removes my panties, she turns to the doctor that just stepped into the room. "She just miscarried. The fetus appears to be intact."

"Chloe, I'm Dr. Nolan. I'm so sorry for your loss. I need to examine you to make sure your body got rid of everything, okay?"

All I can do is nod as a strange numbness comes over me.

***

I can hear the hushed voices, but I refuse to open my eyes. I'm not ready to see the looks of pity on their faces. She's gone, my little girl is gone, and I feel so fucking empty. I feel like a part of my soul is gone. I'd barely gotten used to the idea of being someone's mom, and now it doesn't matter. Nothing matters anymore.

Stacy held me while they did the examination, and I got lucky and didn't need a D&C. They told me if the bleeding doesn't stop that I might have to have one, but we'll just have to wait and see. I gave them permission to take my baby to the lab and see if they could find any abnormalities that may have caused the miscarriage.

My Tay Tay cried right along with me when they let me look at my baby. She looked perfect, just super tiny.

After I was discharged, my dad pushed me in the wheelchair, and Pops held my hand. They tried to get me to make small talk, but I didn't want to talk. I just wanted to go home, shower, then crawl into my bed and fall into oblivion, which brings me to now.

Ragnar and Lagertha are both snuggled up under the covers, providing me with their emotional support. Yes, they're only cats, but they're my babies and can sense that I'm hurting. Ragnar is curled against my chest, and Laggie is curled up against my stomach, like she knows.

Tears leak from my eyes, and I don't bother wiping them away. All I keep thinking is I did something wrong. Maybe I ate something I shouldn't have. What if it was because of the cats?

I feel the bed compress but keep my eyes closed. My hope is they go away. "Chloe? Do you need anything?" It's Dad. "Baby girl, talk to me. I know you're awake." He sits there saying nothing until finally he sighs. "I'll be in the living room if you need anything."

The click of the door lets me know that I'm alone. Thank God.

Chapter Six

Joe

After stepping inside my apartment, the first thing I do is take a shower. It was a bad fucking night. I made a DUI arrest, and the guy resisted, elbowing me in the face. Once I got the perp to the station, he puked all over me. Even though I had a shower at the station, I can still smell it. I strip out of my clothes on my way to the bathroom and spend a good thirty minutes in scalding hot water, soaping myself multiple times.

Climbing out, I wrap a towel around my waist and make some coffee. While that's brewing, I throw on a t-shirt and a pair of cut-off sweats. I reach the living room as a knock sounds at my door. It's only seven thirty in the morning; I can't imagine who it could be. Looking through the peephole, I see it's my dad and Uncle Dustin.

Pulling open the door, I smile. "Hey guys, what are you doing here?" My smile fades immediately when I see the look on their faces. "What's wrong?"

"Can we come in?" I step back, and my dad walks in first, followed by my uncle. "Son, come sit down."

I follow them and sit in my recliner. "What's going on? You're starting to freak me out."

I figure Dad has something to say to me, but instead it's my uncle. "Your aunt went with her mom to Atlanta to celebrate Chloe's dad's birthday. During the party, Chloe started bleeding and then cramping really bad. I hate to be the one to tell you, but she lost the baby."

A strange buzzing starts in my ears. She lost the baby; she lost *our* baby. The baby I was too scared to deal with. Without thinking, I grab my end table, shit flying everywhere, and throw it against my flat screen. My dad and uncle grab me and push me back into the chair.

Tears begin to run down my face. I don't even bother trying to hide them. "How is— is she?"

"She's not doing too good. Your aunt says she's not talking to anyone. Chloe consented to have the baby tested to find out if there were any abnormalities, so at least she'll have some sort of answer." My uncle's hand is on my shoulder.

"What was it?" They look at me with a questioning look. "A girl or a boy?"

"It was a girl. I'm so sorry, Joe."

I bury my face in my hands. My palms are wet from the tears that have begun to fall again. There is such a painful ache in my chest right now. This is my fault; I did this. If I would've been involved, that would've eased her stress. I wipe my face and look at my dad. "This is my fault. I got scared and told her I didn't want to be involved." I suck in a breath. "It was a lie. I wanted that baby—I swear to you I did."

My dad lays his hand on my other shoulder. "You were scared, and that's okay. This is not your fault. This isn't her fault, either."

I push up out of my chair. "I need to go to Atlanta. I need to see her."

In my room, I grab my duffle bag and start shoving clothes into it. "Son, what about your job?"

"I'll stop by the station and talk to my boss. I haven't taken any time off or called in sick. I think I'm allowed to take time off for an emergency. Whether Chloe wants me or not, she's going to need me." My dad follows me into the bathroom, where I grab my toiletries.

"Son, why don't you wait a few days? There's a good chance that she won't want to see you right now." He's right, and I'm being selfish, but I don't care.

"Too bad. That was my child, too."

My dad sighs. "Son, I just want you prepared. As far as she knows, you didn't want the baby."

I hang my head because as much as he's right, I have to go. I just do. Slinging my bag over my shoulder, I walk into the living room where my uncle is cleaning up the mess I made. "Thanks," I tell him.

"I texted your aunt and told her you were coming. She's not sure that's a good idea."

I take a frustrated breath. "No disrespect, but I don't care if she thinks it's not a good idea. I need to see Chloe—end of story." I grab my wallet and phone, shoving them both in my pocket. "Lock up on your way out," I holler as I head toward the front door.

"Joe, please reconsider. At least wait until tomorrow. You shouldn't drive right now." My dad moves to stand right in front of me. "I know you're hurting and you want to support Chloe while she deals with this loss, but driving while you're upset is not safe, and you should know that."

"Dad, I promise you I'm fine. Yes, I'm upset, but I'm okay."

"Okay, so you're okay, but you just got off the night shift. Sleep for a couple of hours first, at least."

Honestly, I'm fine—I'll sleep when I check into a hotel, and that's what I tell them.

"Fine, but I want periodic phone calls and a call when you get there. Your mother will worry."

"Yeah, okay." I reach for the door, but he stops me with a hand on my arm. "What?"

"I'm not sure what you're expecting to have happen when you get there, but whatever it is, I just want you happy." He pulls me into a back-slapping hug. As much as we've fought over the years, I love my dad. He's always stood behind every decision I've made.

"Thanks. I love you." I head out the door, jump in my car, and head to Chloe.

On my way out of town, I stop at the gas station and buy a jumbo cup of crappy coffee; two stale, dry donuts; a pack of gum; and a huge bottle of water. In the car, I call my boss. Chief Jones is probably at the station already. The man has been with the Beaufort Police Department for twenty years, and it was after he came and gave a talk at my high school that I started considering joining the police force.

His secretary answers, and he's there so she puts me right back to him. I tell him about Chloe and the baby and that I need to take some time off to see to her. Of course he's cool about it. "I'm so sorry, son."

"Thank you."

"Take as much time as you need. You don't qualify for FMLA, but you can take a leave of absence," he says.

"I don't think I'll be gone for more than a week, but I'll keep you posted." I take a deep breath. "Thanks for being so understanding."

"My wife and I lost a child. She was only eight weeks along, but we still felt it. Just be patient with her. Take care."

We hang up, and I toss my phone in the seat. His words replay in my head, and I know I need to heed them. There's a good chance she won't want to see me, and I'm prepared for that. My mom has always said I'm stubborn, which means I won't give up.

***

After checking into my hotel for the night, I take the elevator up and stick the card in the door, waiting for the little beep. Stepping into the room, I drop my bag on the floor and collapse on the bed. I fall asleep immediately.

My eyes flutter open, and it takes me a second to

remember where I am. Then it hits me like a ton of bricks. Chloe…Baby…Miscarriage. The heaviness returns as I grab my phone and look at the time. "Shit." It's four in the morning. I slept the entire day away. Flinging myself back on the bed, I stare at the ceiling, my eyes getting used to the dark.

I end up lying in bed until the sun shines brightly in my room. It's seven now, and I think I even dozed off for a little bit on and off. I climb out of bed, strip out of my clothes, and take a shower.

I throw on a pair of tan cargo shorts and a blue t-shirt. After stuffing my wallet and my phone into my pockets, I slip on my tennis shoes and head downstairs to grab some breakfast.

It's a buffet, so I grab my plate and pile it high with food. I grab a cup of coffee and carry it over to a single-seat table. Digging in immediately, I didn't realize just how hungry I was, and even though the food isn't that great, it's at least something.

I feel eyes on me and look up to find two women around my age openly checking me out. Normally, I'd be all over them and in about five minutes we'd be upstairs having a good time. Instead I give them a chin lift and go back to eating my food.

Chloe's always on my mind these days, and until I see her and we talk, there's no way I can be with someone else. It would feel wrong. How come being with Chloe feels right? Maybe it's just lust. We had amazing chemistry our night together. Her body fit against mine like it was designed specifically for me. Fuck, I can still taste her on my tongue.

Fuck, what am I doing? Chloe just lost our baby,

and I'm thinking about fucking her? I shake my head because I'm clearly a horny idiot.

After I finish eating, I pop some gum in my mouth and head out to the parking lot. I climb into my car and drive the five minutes to her place.

I reach my destination: a cute little white home. It's surrounded by trees and shrubbery, giving it a cozy feel. Her Camaro is in the driveway with a silver two-door Mini Cooper behind it. I take a deep breath and climb out of my car. I make my way up to the door. Lifting my hand to knock, I jerk back because the door flings open and her friend Eli stands there.

He glowers at me and doesn't say anything, but I do. "I need to see her."

Eli closes the front door and steps onto the front porch. "You don't need to see shit. She doesn't want to see *us*, so I can be certain that she does not want to see *you*." His finger is in my face.

"That was my baby, too." I take a step forward, brushing his hand away. "I'm *going* to go inside and see for myself how she's doing. You can try to stop me, but I'm an officer of the law, so trust me, you don't want to test me." I feel my stomach lurch as Eli's eyes widen in shock. *Holy shit, did I just threaten Chloe's best friend?* I take a deep breath. "Fuck, I'm sorry, man, but I need to see her. *Please.*"

He narrows his eyes but nods and moves out of the way, letting me push the door open and step inside. I don't even take the opportunity to look around her house, even though I didn't get a chance to really wander around the last time I was here. I was too focused on her.

At the end of the hall, I reach her bedroom door. I slowly open it and peer inside. She's in bed, because I can see her dark hair peeking out from her comforter. "Go away, Eli. I don't want to talk."

I step farther into her bedroom and shut her door. "It's me."

Even with her buried under piles of blankets, I can still see her body go stiff. Ragnar crawls out from under the comforter and sits on the end of the bed, staring at me. I ignore the giant cat and come around to the side of the bed so I can see her.

I pull up the blanket, and Chloe tries to hide her face. Her skin's fair enough already, but now she's pale with purplish bags standing out under her bloodshot eyes. "Why are you here?" Her voice is scratchy and hoarse.

My hand makes its way under the blankets until it connects with hers. She tries to pull it away from me, but I don't let her. I don't get on the bed, but I get down on my knees next to it. I'm tall enough that I can lean in close to her. "I'm so fucking sorry." Tears slip from her eyes, and I reach out, wiping them away. My own eyes feel that ache that happens before tears fall.

"What are you sorry for?" she snaps. "You didn't want her."

Pain slices through me, and I clench my eyes shut so she doesn't see the hurt. It's not her fault, though. I deserved that, and I take it. "That's the thing. I *did* want her. I wanted her more than you could ever know. I was just scared." I stroke her cheek, and she lets me. "I'm going to regret that for the rest of my life."

"I keep thinking about everything I've done. If maybe something I did caused this to happen." I open my mouth to speak, but she shakes her head. "I know I didn't, but it doesn't make it hurt any less."

Neither of us says anything for a long time. Finally her eyes start to look heavy. "Thank you for coming," she whispers right before her eyes drift shut. I don't make a move to stand until her soft snores fill the room.

Slowly I stand and then head out into the living room, where Eli and now Carter are waiting. Carter stands and comes toward me. I'll kick his ass if he tries anything; I don't care if he's almost as big as I am. He stops in front of me. "How was she?"

"Sad. Weepy. She just fell asleep." I don't miss Carter's look of surprise.

"She's sleeping?" I nod. "Thank fuck. She didn't sleep last night. She'll pretend, but as soon as she thinks we're gone, she opens her eyes."

"When I stepped out, she was snoring."

Carter steps past me and disappears down the hall. He comes back a few seconds later and looks at Eli. "She's out. I'm talking drool and everything." He looks back at me. "What did you do?"

"Nothing, just told her that I was sorry and that I wanted the baby. I was scared, and she let me hold her hand while she talked. She thanked me for coming, and then her eyes closed."

Carter excuses himself, and I can hear him talking to their parents. I'm glad she's sleeping. It hurts to think that she's suffering as hard as she seems to be. I'd love to take credit for her finally sleeping, but it was probably just exhaustion catching up with her.

Once Carter comes back into the living room, I ask both him and Eli to give me some time alone with her. "I don't intend on hurting her. I just think we should talk, spend time together."

"Fine, but only because I have to work in the morning." He moves until we're nose to nose. "If you hurt her, I don't care if you're a cop—I will end you." Carter turns on his heel and heads over to Eli. "Let's go. We're not too far away if she needs us."

They both just look at me as they head to the front door and out. I move toward the front window and watch them walk to their cars. After they're gone, I step out to my own car, grab my bag, and bring it inside. I brought it just in case I ended up staying at her place.

I want her to get as much sleep as possible, giving her body a chance to heal itself. I put my bag in her bedroom against the wall and then step back out. A loud meow sounds from behind me. I scoop Ragnar up in my arms, and his purr vibrates against my chest.

"Hey, boy. Your momma is going to be okay. She just needs a little time, okay?"

That cat again answers me. I set him down and find a bag of treats. I grab him one, and he sits on his hind legs while he waits. She must sense them because Lagertha comes out a few seconds later and sits the same way. I find the remote for Chloe's TV, turn it on, and then turn it way down. Flipping through the channels, I stop on a show about cars.

A while later, my phone dings. I pick it up and see it's a text from Vi.

Violet: Hey you. I talked to Mom. I'm so sorry.

Joe: Thanks.

Violet: Mom says you're there. How is she?

Joe: She's finally sleeping. I just don't know what to do or say to her.

Violet: Talk to Carrington or Damien. They miscarried before the twins, remember?

I totally forgot that my cousin and her husband had lost a baby. My aunt Bellamy, Carrington's mom, also lost a baby, but she was toward the end of her pregnancy when it happened. Maybe they'd both be willing to talk to Chloe. Then she'd know that it's possible to go on and have healthy children.

Joe: That's right. Maybe I'll give them a call. How are you?

She's pregnant, too, so I'm sure all of this can't make her feel good.

Violet: I'm great! I feel good. Of course now I feel guilty because you both are going through your loss.

Joe: No, don't feel bad. I'm happy for you guys. It hurts Vi—it hurts fucking bad.

My phone rings, and I quickly answer it. "Hey."

"I know it hurts. I'm so freaking sorry. Do you want me to fly up there? I could come see you both."

"As much as I would love to see you right now, I just don't think it would be a good idea. You're pregnant, and I'm afraid it could upset Chloe to see you."

"Oh God, you're right. What was I thinking?"

"You were thinking about your cousin and...well, your cousin." It's too bad she wasn't closer; I could use my best friend.

We don't talk much longer before hanging up. Quietly, I walk down the hall and peek in on Chloe. Her quiet snores fill the room. I move around her bed, reach out, and stroke her hair out of her face. Even though she's got bags under her eyes and she's pale, she's still fucking gorgeous.

She doesn't even move.

Chapter Seven

Chloe

My eyes feel like there's sand in them; that's what I get for falling asleep with my contacts in. The sun is shining brightly into my bedroom, which normally doesn't happen until the late afternoon. I fling my blankets back and gingerly sit up. It takes me a minute before I've got my wits about me, and I stand up. I feel a warm tiny gush, and then I remember what happened.

With tears leaking from my eyes, I step across the hall into the bathroom, shutting the door behind me. I use the toilet and take the soiled pad out of my panties. They told me I'd bleed, but dammit I just wanted it to magically be over so I could try to forget any of this ever happened. It hurts too much to think about.

I start the shower, and while it gets hot, I brush my teeth because it feels like I have a layer of scum on them. I do the whole mouthwash and floss thing and then strip out of my pajamas. When I step into the shower, the hot water feels good all over my sore, tired body.

I wash and condition my hair and then scrub my body clean. Running the soapy washcloth over my stomach, I freeze. The tiny little pooch I had is gone. A sob tears from my throat as I drop to my knees. Why? I just want someone to tell me why I lost my baby.

What I wouldn't give to have been able to see her alive. To hold her in my arms and smell her sweet baby scent. The tears slow, but the emptiness I feel is crushing.

The water shuts off, and my head jerks up to find Joe standing there with a towel, concern written all over his face. He doesn't say anything—he just wraps the towel around me and then stands me up, hugging me to his chest before he proceeds to dry me off. He grabs one of my pads and leads me back into my room. He grabs me panties, sweats, and a t-shirt.

"Get dressed, babe. I'll be right back." He steps into the bathroom while I quickly put the pad in my panties and then slip them on. I'm just slipping my t-shirt on when he comes back into my room with a hairbrush. "Come with me." Joe grabs my hand, leads me out into my living room, and sits me on my ottoman with my back to him.

Slowly he starts to use the brush to work out the tangles. When he's done brushing it, he surprises me when he braids it, and quickly. "Where did you learn to braid?"

"Between my baby sister and niece, I've become quite proficient in braids, ponytails, and buns. Are you hungry?" I shake my head. "Let's at least get you something small. You haven't had anything. You were asleep for a long time."

That's when I look at the clock and see that I slept about five hours. "I'm not hungry. You can leave now. I don't need you here." This isn't like me, but I can't help the venom that spews from my mouth. "Get out." I shove him, but he doesn't budge.

"I'm not leaving you."

"You didn't want her, and now I can't have her." I know my accusatory tone is uncalled for, but it's like I don't have control of my mouth. It's not connected to my brain. "You're off the hook. You got what you wanted." I regret the words as soon as they leave my mouth. Joe looks like I've slapped him. He's so hurt right now.

I open my mouth to apologize, but his hand slashes through the air. "I don't want to hear anything else you have to say." He leans in close. "You don't know shit."

Before I register what's happened, he disappears down the hall and returns with his bag and then my front door is slamming shut and headlights shine into my living room. My feet become unglued, and I run to the door, throwing it open. By the time I reach my driveway, he's flying down the street.

Guilt, shame, and regret fill me as I head back inside. I grab my phone and call him. It goes straight to voicemail. "Joe, please call me. I need to know you're okay. I am so sorry. That was mean and uncalled for and so not true. I was hurting, and I needed to hurt someone else, and you were the unlucky victim. It's no excuse." My voice breaks. "We both lost her. I don't know you very well, but you just don't seem like the type of guy who would've stayed gone long." I inhale. "Please call me."

I dial my parents, and it's Pops who answers. "Hey, baby girl."

"D-Daddy. Please come o-over." My words are broken by tears as I remember the horrid things I said.

"Chloe, what is it, baby? Dad said Joe was with you."

I tell him that he was, but now I need my pops. He tells me he's heading out now and will be here soon. He'll know what to do.

I see his headlights and move toward the door, opening it as he reaches the steps. I rush right into his arms. With his arms around me, he leads me into the house.

***

A week has gone by, and Joe won't answer or return my calls. I even had Tay Tay try and talk to him for me, but she was rebuffed too. It's my fault, and I deserve this. This is my punishment.

Physically, I've healed up well from the miscarriage. I'm just spotting now, and soon I know it'll be gone and I'll be back to normal. My heart and my mind aren't even close to being healed, though. Truth is…I haven't been able to stop thinking about Joe. The look on his face haunts me. We both lost something so precious, and I threw it in his face that he got scared. I'm such an awful, horrible bitch.

Closing my eyes, I take a deep breath, clearing my head. I go back to polishing the locket I just got done engraving. It's for a father from his daughter on her wedding day.

Pain hits my chest when I think about my dad and when he realized the other day that he was still wearing the grandpa pendant I made for his birthday. His face paled, and he yanked it from his neck, shoving it in his pocket.

I'd walked up to him. "You better keep it, because one day you'll need it." His face had softened, and his eyes had turned glassy.

I place the locket in the velvet box and shut the lid. "Chloe?" I turn my head and find Hailey standing next to me. Since I came back to work the other day, she's been surprisingly friendly.

"Yeah?"

She wrings her hands together in front of her. "I'm running across the street to get a coffee. Would you like one?"

"No coffee, but I'll take an Earl Grey, please." I grab a five out of my pocket and hand it over to her. "Thanks."

Hailey takes the money and disappears out the door. Mr. Harmon comes through the doors from the front of the store and sits down next to me. He knows what happened and had sent a lovely bouquet of flowers while I was home recovering. "How're you doing being back? Do you need anything?"

"I'm good. Glad to be busy. Thank you again for

the flowers."

"You're welcome, honey. Uh…Hailey knows about your miscarriage. She overheard me talking to your dad. I'm so sorry." His brow is furrowed and his mouth pinched tight.

That explains the odd behavior. I grab his hands. "It's okay—I promise. She's actually been very nice, so maybe you did me a favor."

"Well, I'm here if you ever need me." He squeezes my hands before standing up and returning out front.

A few minutes later, Hailey returns and hands me my tea, a little bag, and my change. "In the bag is lemon, sugar, and cream. I wasn't sure what you liked."

I give the first genuine smile I think I've ever given her, or at least since I first started and before I figured out what a bitch she was. "I like cream and sugar. Thanks again." After doctoring up my tea, I take a sip.

"My sister lost a baby." Hailey sits down across from me. "I don't know exactly what you're going through, but I know what it's like watching someone you love while they're hurting. My sister belongs to this group. It's other women who've suffered miscarriages, too. They just talk about their feelings and how they deal with stuff." She pulls a card out of her purse and hands it to me. "That's where they meet and the days and times. My sister said there's no pressure, but if you need to talk, they're all great listeners."

I don't even know what to say right now except, "Thank you. I'll seriously consider it." She gives me a genuine smile before standing up, but I stop her with a hand on her arm. "Does your sister have kids now?"

"She's got three now. One was before and two were after." That makes me feel a little better but not much.

"I'll consider going. Thanks."

***

I sit in my car, my stomach turning. Why am I scared to go in? I've never met a stranger, and it's always been that way. Now I'm not sure if I can go in or not. I haven't told my parents, my brother, or Eli that I'm doing this. I didn't want to get their hopes up if I chickened out and didn't go.

Taking a deep breath, I climb out and make my way inside. On an easel is a chalkboard, and it says,

Over the Rainbow After Angel Babies.

There are at least ten women sitting in a circle. The one who seems to be the leader spots me and stands up, waving me over.

"Welcome. I'm Elizabeth. How long ago was your loss?"

"T-Two weeks. Hailey sent me."

Elizabeth smiles at me. "That's my baby sister. You must be Chloe. She said you might come. Here, come sit by me."

I do as she says, and my eyes drift around the room. There are women of all ages and races here. They're all giving me the smile of understanding.

My eyes burn, and I rapidly blink back the tears that threaten to spill.

Only a few of the women actually speak today, but that's because no one tells them to stop. They're able to speak and work through whatever they need to. The first woman had been just seventeen when she lost her baby. She'd felt guilty for thinking it was a blessing since she was young and single. Now at thirty-five, she's a mom to three boys, but she still thinks about the baby she lost.

Each story is different but the same, and I'm glad to know that I'm not alone and it's possible to go on to have healthy, happy babies. Maybe there's hope for me, too.

After the meeting, everyone leaves but Elizabeth and an African-American woman. "Chloe, this is Reggie. Reggie helped me form this group three years ago."

I shake her hand. "Nice to meet you, Reggie."

"You too. Do you have time to have a cup of coffee with us?"

I agree and follow them up to the counter and order myself a vanilla latte. Once I have my beverage in hand, I follow them to a table and sit down. "Tell us about yourself."

I hate being put on the spot, but I knew this was going to happen when they asked me for coffee. "Well, I'm thirty-one. Single. I'm a jewelry designer at Harmon's. I also do some designs that I sell on my own. My brother and our best friends are all in a band together. I sing lead vocals and play the piano. My brother is the drummer. Umm…we're biological brother and sister but were adopted by our dads." I've never and will never hide the fact that I have two dads from anyone.

Reggie leans forward, and I'm worried she's going to ask me something inappropriate, but instead she surprises me. "Was it hard for you to date as a teenager with two dads and a brother?"

"Oh my gosh, yes. If my dad liked the kid, my pops hated him and vice versa. My brother had the ones he tolerated and the ones he tormented." They both smile and laugh. They ask to see some of my designs, so I pull up the pictures. Elizabeth coincidentally owns a little boutique by one of the clubs we play at a lot.

"Bring some pieces by and we'll see if maybe we can't sell some for you on consignment."

"Sure, that'd be great. Thanks." They tell me a little bit about themselves, and then we all head out.

As I drive back toward my place, I feel better than when I left…a little bit.

Chapter Eight

Joe

I grab two pairs of jeans, a couple of t-shirts, and socks and underwear, stuffing them in my overnight bag. I shove my shaving kit that also has my shampoo and body wash in there on top of my clothes. The box of condoms on my bed taunts me. Is this really what I want? To go out and have random sex with women I don't know? Before Chloe, I'd have no problem, but now—shit, now I don't know what I want. I'm only making this trip because Chris, one of my good buddies from back in the day, begged me to come, and my dad thought it would be good for me to get out.

We're going up to Atlanta to hit some bars and see some bands play. Chris has made it his mission to get me laid and out of this perpetual funk I've been in. I never told him about Chloe or the baby, which means he has no clue why I'm in the funk.

My mom has been hovering like crazy, and I know she means well, but I'm fine, or at least that's what I tell everyone. She's tried to encourage me to date or at least meet new people, but it hasn't interested me. Not when a raven-haired beauty seems to monopolize all my thoughts. Truth is, I've been torturing myself every day for the past month listening to every single voicemail that Chloe's left me.

I could hear the regret and the sincerity of her apologies in each message, but I just wasn't sure about what I was going to say. Then more and more time went by, and I just assumed it was too late. Especially since last week, her calls stopped coming. I can't say I blame her for not calling anymore. I wouldn't if I were her.

The roar of motorcycles outside lets me know that Chris and the boys are here. I throw the strap of my bag over my shoulder, and on the way out I grab my helmet, riding glasses, and leather jacket just in case.

I greet everybody and walk over to my Dyna Glide. First, I shove my leather coat into my saddle bag and bungie my bag to the back of my bike. The sun is shining down on me as I strap my low-profile dot helmet on and my aviators. As soon as my bike starts, the familiar rumble makes my stress just disappear.

As soon as we hit I-75, I'm able to hit the throttle, and then it's smooth sailing. The wind in my face and the sun shining down on me are the perfect cures for the case of the blues I seem to have.

We hit Atlanta shortly after three, so we head over to our hotel. We splurged and got a couple of suites with two rooms just in case we brought anyone back. Plus it's not often that I can get away like this for the weekend.

We decide to get ready and then go grab dinner before heading over to the Tabernacle Theater for the concert. It's all local bands that were voted on by their fans. It'll either be amazing or it'll suck. Obviously, I hope it's the former, because that would really suck to get that kind of opportunity and then to fucking blow it.

I check myself out in the mirror. My black hair is shaved close to my scalp on the sides and a little longer on top. My face is covered in a light five o'clock shadow so I just trimmed it up a bit. I'm wearing a black button-up shirt with the sleeves rolled up on my forearms. It's tucked into some boot-cut jeans. I slip on my black motorcycle boots. I dab a little cologne on and then head out into the living room.

***

Leaning against the bar, I scope out the women. There's a lot here tonight. I take a swig of my beer while hoping that one of these women piques my interest enough for me to take her back to the hotel. With a sigh, I head back over to where my group is seated. A few women have been circling them, hoping to get invited over.

I see, as I walk up, that Chris already has a cute little redhead in his lap, their heads real close as they talk. Leaning against the tall table, I wait for the next band to come out.

101

"Hi." I turn my head and spot a really cute blonde standing next to me. I feel no interest whatsoever, but maybe if I fake it, it'll naturally kick in.

"Hey. I'm Joe." I hold out my hand to her.

"Hailey." She places her soft hand in mine. "Are you from around here?"

I shake my head. "South Carolina. Just up here for a guy's weekend. You?"

"Born and raised in Athens. What have you thought about the bands so far?" She leans against the table and smiles up at me.

"They've been great."

"The next band you're really going to like. They're called Beautiful Rage. They do a lot of covers but put their twists on the songs." She turns to look at the stage and then back to me. "Oh…here they come now."

The stage is dark, but I can see people moving around. The lights in the whole place go down, and everyone stops talking. All eyes are on the stage, waiting to see what's happening.

A lone female voice starts carrying through the speakers, and I'm mesmerized. Her voice is raspy yet melodic. I recognize the lyrics. The song is from that vampire movie that Abby used to make me watch with her.

Her voice fades, and the crowd starts cheering and clapping. The energy is explosive, and just as the lights kick on, the instruments start to play. When the spotlight shines on the singer, I'm struck speechless. I've heard Chloe sing before, but right now I'm in serious awe. She's mesmerizing, and as

I look around, it's easy to see I'm not the only one.

The song ends, and she grabs the microphone out of the stand. "How y'all doing tonight? For those of you who don't know us, we're Beautiful Rage." People scream and clap. "Let's say we cut the chitchat. Are you ready to rock?" she shouts into the microphone.

She's wearing an old and faded Mötley Crüe t-shirt that hangs off one shoulder, exposing the creamy expanse of her skin and the elegant line of her neck. The shirt is tied, showing off her small waist. The jeans she's wearing are old, worn, and faded. They mold perfectly to her ass and make my dick hard.

Hailey tugs on my arm and leans toward me. "I work with the singer. Her name's Chloe. She's so talented, but she's pathetic." She doesn't notice my body stiffening. "She was pregnant but lost it. She's in my sister's support group, and she just goes on and on about hurting the dad or some shit. My sister says she's a fucking bummer. I told her about the group because I was trying to be nice, but God, pathetic much?"

I swear it's taking all my self-control not to lose it on this bitch. It would kill Chloe, no doubt, because I'm sure she's going to the support group to heal. "That's not very nice."

She doesn't even have the decency to look embarrassed or remorseful. "You don't know this girl. Our boss loves her…counts on her more even though I've been there longer. Then she's pregnant and again everyone is up her ass, but then she loses it. I figure I feel bad, bad enough that I'm nice to

103

her. I share that my sister has a group that could help her. Ugh…fucking loser."

"Can you excuse me? I'm running to the bathroom." I make my escape, and Chris looks at me with questioning eyes. I just shake my head and keep moving. On the opposite side of the room, I grab a beer and find a spot to stand. She looks so fucking beautiful up there. I can see why their band was nominated; they have an amazing stage presence.

They sing three more songs, and then they're done. I make my way toward the side of the stage. I need to see her, to talk to her. Fuck, I need to hold her. The security in this place is lacking, because I easily slip past the two guards that are back there.

I reach the lounge, and there are people everywhere. I recognize a couple of the bands that have already played, but I don't want to talk to any of them. My eyes drift around the room until I spot her. She's sitting on a bench by herself staring out the window.

"Oh no. You're not fucking here." I turn to see Eli moving toward me. "You need to go."

At this point, I don't care. He's not going to stop me. "Eli, out of my way. You can't keep me from her." The look on my face must show I'm not playing, because he steps to the side. I reach her, and she must feel me walk up because she turns, her eyes widening comically.

"J-Joe? What are you doing here?" She slowly stands, turning to fully face me.

Is it just me, or is she a little thinner than before? Her porcelain skin looks even paler, if that's possible. Without thinking, I reach out, brushing her hair back from her face. I don't think she knows how expressive her eyes are, but it sucks when she forces her face to go blank so I can't see the emotion in them. "You were beautiful up there tonight."

Her cheeks turn an adorable shade of pink. "Thanks, but what are you doing here?"

"Some buddies and I rode our bikes up for a guy's weekend. I had no clue I was going to see you, but I'm glad I am. Do you want to grab a drink or something?" We need this, whether it's closure or something else.

"Do you think that's a good idea? I said hurtful things…"

"I think it's a great fucking idea. What do you say?" I wait impatiently for an answer. Even though I feel eyes on me, I don't dare look away from her.

She nods her head. "Okay, yeah I am kind of hungry." She picks up her bag and puts the strap across her body. "I just need to tell my brother I'm going. I'll take an Uber or taxi home."

"No, I'll take you home." My bossy tone surprises us both.

"O-Okay…I'll be right back." My eyes follow her movement through the crowd until she reaches Carter and Eli. Eli is staring daggers at me, but I don't give a fuck. Chloe stops next to her friend and kisses his cheek. Although I know Eli is gay, I still don't like his lips on Chloe. *What the fuck?* I'm losing it.

She comes back to me, and the girl who was just smiling at her brother and friend is gone—now she seems tense…worried.

I grab her hand in mine and lead her out of the lounge. There's another band playing so it's loud as hell as I lead her through the hall. I've had a few beers, but I've sipped the last few, drinking water as well. I'll be good to drive after we eat.

Outside, she tries to pull her hand from mine, but I hold firm. We walk silently down the street together until we reach a little bar and grille. It's surprisingly quiet in there, and we grab a table in the corner away from others.

The waitress comes by and takes our orders and then disappears. "How have you been?" She plays nervously with the necklace around her neck.

I reach across the table and pull her hand away from it. "I've been okay. Have you felt all right?"

She nods. "I had my follow up, and they said that when I'm ready I should have no problems conceiving children." The waitress returns with our drinks and fried mushrooms. "Joe, what I said…God, that was so fucking mean and so wrong." She sucks in a breath, and I hate to see her beating herself up.

I get up and slide in next to her. I hug her close as she cries into my shirt. "Shhh…No crying, okay?" She looks up at me, her blue eyes shining bright. I wipe away the tears. "I know you didn't mean it. Yes, it hurt, and I was upset, but I forgive you…okay?"

She buries her head in my chest and nods. "Thank you for being so…so, I don't know. Thank you for being so awesomely sweet."

"Confession?" She nods. "I listened to your

voicemails all the time. I just wanted to hear your voice. Now enough serious stuff—let's eat."

I choose not to move from my spot next to her. My arm finds its way around her shoulder, pulling her close into my side. I want to ask her about the support group or at least tell her what that bitch who works with her said. All of my instincts are telling me that she needs to avoid that group of women like the plague.

I don't give a fuck that they've suffered too, because Chloe probably felt safe sharing her feelings there, and unbeknownst to her, they've betrayed that trust.

"How's your family? I heard Violet's having a girl."

"Yep, everyone's pretty stoked about it but trying hard not to get too excited in front of me." Our daughters would've been close like Vi and I are. *Fuck, is it ever going to stop hurting?*

"Both of my dads walked around on eggshells after they told me. I just wanted to scream that I can be happy for them and sad too, you know? My God, it's sometimes suffocating. Will I ever fully be over it? No, but don't treat me like I'm a fragile piece of glass that could shatter at any moment." She grabs a mushroom and pops it into her mouth. "Tell me about your job. I don't know any cops."

"I've always been on the fence about becoming one, but my sister's husband is one, and that was what gave me the final push to do it. I'd taken criminal justice classes, which helped when I went into the academy. Whatever you believe it's like to be an officer, it's probably not even close. I guess it

107

does depend on which shift you work, too. Second and third shift see more action than first."

Our waitress brings our burgers. I hate moving my arm from around her, but I kind of need them both to eat. Conversation stalls at first while we both dig in. Chloe moans around the huge bite she just took, and I swear my dick is half hard. What is wrong with me? I should've jerked off earlier, and maybe now I wouldn't have this problem.

Seeing her and talking to her again was supposed to be our chance to get closure, so why does that fucking hurt? Why does the idea of never seeing her again make my chest ache?

"This is the best burger I've ever eaten," Chloe says, pulling my attention back to her. "I don't think I've ever eaten here."

We finish eating, and as soon as we slide out of the booth, she surprises me by slipping her hand in mine. Hand in hand, we make our way out of the bar. It's ten o'clock and still warm outside. It's the perfect weather to go for a ride.

I step in front of her. "Do you want to go for a ride on my bike?"

"Really?" I nod. "Yes, please! I haven't been on a bike since my dad sold his. It's the perfect night for a ride." Her smile is radiant. I can't stop myself before I grab her by her face and kiss her lips, slowly and thoroughly. Her tongue immediately seeks mine, and it tangles with hers.

Reluctantly, I pull away—we're in public, and this wasn't supposed to be what we're doing. Weren't we supposed to be getting closure on whatever it was that we had? I ignore those thoughts as we reach the Ritz. They only offer valet parking, but they did let us park our bikes ourselves.

I back mine out of my space and then put my stand back down. I grab my helmet and my spare, slipping hers on for her. She looks fucking sexy as hell with that helmet on. I grab her the spare riding glasses I have, and then she's all set. When I do the same, I climb on and then hold my hand out to her. She hops on like she's done it a million times.

Chloe wraps her arms around my waist as I start my bike. Her hands rest on my waist as I slowly pull out of the parking lot. We drive around town, and the wind kicks up her sweet scent, and it wraps around me. Her tits are pressed up against my back, and it's turning me the fuck on. I think of anything other than Chloe or her hot body: my mom, my sisters, and Natalie.

Thank God that works. We don't go anywhere—we just ride. We only get to talk at stoplights. She tells me about a jewelry line she's working on and about her band. Her breath hits me in small minty puffs.

We pull up in front of her house. I take off my helmet and glasses and do the same for her, stowing them in my saddlebags.

Hand in hand, we walk up to her door. "Would you like to come in?"

With my free hand, I reach out and tuck her hair behind her ear. "Yeah."

I let go of her hand, and she lets us into her house. We're greeted by some angry cats. They're both sitting next to the sofa and look at their mom with the same expression. "Hi, my babies. Are you mad Mommy left you?"

Damn if those damn cats don't answer her, "Meow." She squats down in front of them and gives them both scratches on the head. Ragnar stares at me like I'm scum, but maybe because in his eyes I am. I follow Chloe as she stands up and walks into the kitchen. She grabs a bag of treats and throws a couple down in front of the furry pair.

The scent of lemon hits my nose, and that's when I see she's adding drops of oil to her diffuser. Sadness hits me when I think about the last time I saw it. I had put peppermint oil in it while she slept to hopefully ward off the terrible morning sickness she'd had.

"Joe? Hey, what is it?" I feel her hands touch my face. "Honey, what is it?"

"I am so sorry."

Chloe's arms wrap around me and pull me into a hug. "I'm sorry, too. We're going to get through this, and we'll never forget her." Chloe had left me a voicemail after the results from the test they did on our baby, and unfortunately there was nothing that they could find that would cause Chloe to lose her. Did I call her back and offer her comfort? No. I nursed my snit and was an asshole.

"I know, but that's not why I'm sorry. I'm sorry that I wasn't here when you needed me and that you had to heal alone." She pulls back and grabs my hand, pulling me into the living room and then pushing me down on the sofa.

"Hey. It's not your fault. I'm the one who pushed you away—blamed you for it." Chloe places her hand over my heart, and I swear my stupid dick is twitching in my jeans. "I've been going to a support group, and it's really helped." Just the mention of that group has my blood boiling. "What?"

"Tonight, before you came out to play, a blonde came up and started talking to me. We talked for a while and then you came on. She said she worked with you. Chloe, it kills me to say this, but that bitch's sister was talking shit about you. She told her sister stuff that you had talked about."

Chloe moves fast, and before I know it she's off the sofa and marching into the kitchen. Just as I step inside, she starts in on the person whom she just called. "Reggie, it's Chloe." Silence. "Yeah, I know it's late. You tell that bitch, Elizabeth, that she better stay the fuck away from me. I know she's told her sister all about what I've said in our group.

"That group is supposed to be a safe place for us to share our feelings in and a group that supports and uplifts each other. She's ruined that for me, and shame on you if you knew what was going on."

Chloe ends the call and looks at me with fire in her eyes. "I'm sorry she said that shit to me," I say. "I wasn't going to tell you, but the thought of you pouring your heart out to that woman, and for her to tell people, pisses me the fuck off."

"I'm glad you did. Fucking Hailey, she's been a pain in my ass for a while. I'm Mr. Harmon's best designer, and he loves me, so she's jealous, and up until recently she was always nasty to me. I am a hundred percent sure that she's going to be nasty again." She grabs a couple of beers out her refrigerator and hands me one. "I think we could both use one of these." We both twist off our caps and clink our bottles together before taking huge swallows.

She grabs me by my arm and pulls me into the living room. "Do you want to watch a movie?"

"Sure." I sit down, pulling her to sit next to me.

We settle into the sofa, her head resting on my shoulder as we scan Netflix for something to watch. Once we've picked the movie, *Jaws*, I reach over and shut the lamp off. The room is engulfed in darkness, and it's not long before we're both engrossed in the classic.

Chapter Nine

Chloe

My eyes open, and it takes a second for the sleep fog to fade. Why am I so hot? Movement from behind reminds me that Joe slept over last night. I fell asleep halfway through the movie and woke up as Joe was lifting me off the sofa. He was going to go back to the hotel, but I had invited him to stay.

I'm not sure why I did it, because it wasn't really a good idea, but the thought of him leaving didn't sit well with me. We have a connection, and it's not just the baby we lost. There's something there, but I'm just not sure what it is and whether I want to even explore it. He's twenty-four, and I'm thirty-one.

I take a quick shower, making sure I scrub and shave every inch of me that needs it—just in case. After I step out of the shower, I dry off and then throw on my robe. Back in my bedroom, Joe is still asleep, so I quickly moisturize my body before throwing on cut-off sweats and a tank top. I take my

113

hair down and shake it out as I move to my side of the bed and then climb back in.

Joe's arm wraps around me, and he pulls me until I'm snug against his chest. "You smell so good," he whispers against my neck.

A moan slipping from my lips has his hand sliding up under my tank top. He pinches my nipples and then massages my breast. My hips tip back, rubbing against his hard dick. I moan in protest as he removes his hand, but it's only to brush my hair away from my neck so he can place his lips there.

I reach behind me and grab his hand, bringing it around my front and shoving it down my cut-off sweats. His fingers slip through my wetness, and I should be embarrassed but I'm not. Joe's groan vibrates against my back, making goosebumps pop up all over my body. My legs spread enough for him to slip a finger inside of me.

"Fuck, baby, you're so wet for me, aren't you? Are you going to let me fuck you?"

"God yes…Please."

He backs away from me, and for a second I'm worried he's getting out of bed, but instead I'm suddenly on my back. Joe rips my tank top off and then my shorts. I've never had a problem with nudity before. I'm lucky to have a nice body, but he's probably used to girls a lot younger than me—girls who have flawless skin, tighter bodies, and perkier boobs.

My hands move to cover myself, but he grabs them, pinning them by my head. "Don't you dare hide that body from me—you're fucking gorgeous.

Don't move your hands. Understand?" I nod my head slowly and watch as his hands travel down my arms and then slowly move to my breasts.

My back arches, and I moan as his fingers pluck at each nipple. The look in his eyes can only be classified as hungry, the blue so bright my pussy spasms around an invisible cock. His hands travel down, down and down. He dips a finger into my pussy then swirls it around my clit. Joe bends down and sucks a nipple into his mouth just as he thrusts two fingers inside me.

Immediately, I begin to come, and he starts massaging my G-spot. That pressure builds, and then I moan deep and hard as I gush all over his hand. "Fuck. I love when you do that." His mouth moves up my chest until his lips are on mine.

Our kiss is wild and intense, my hands winding around his shoulders. His tongue enters my mouth, and my tongue duels with his. Fuck, he's a good kisser. He removes his fingers while we kiss and then rubs his cock against me. Only the material of his boxer briefs separates us.

I push on his shoulders until he's on his back. I straddle his thighs and stare down at his beautiful chiseled features. Leaning down, I place my lips against his square jaw, biting at the flesh. His grunt spurs me on. My lips travel to his, nipping at the flesh. My hair creates a dark curtain around us.

My hips begin to roll, grinding against his dick. He swallows my moan before he grips my hips and pulls me down harder, putting pressure on my clit. I pant against his lips as the pressure begins to build. "I want to hear you come, baby."

He kisses me hard, and coupled with his cock rubbing my clit just right, I begin to come, crying out against his lips. Joe flips us. "Please tell me you have a condom," he says.

"Top drawer." I reach my arm out, pointing to the nightstand.

He grabs one then quickly tears off his boxer briefs. I take in his gorgeous cock and lick my lips. It's perfection—long but not too long and beautifully thick. My attention goes back to the condom he's tearing open. Joe sheaths himself quickly, and then he's lining himself up with my waiting pussy.

"Hard and fast or slow and easy?"

"Fuck me hard." That's all he needs to hear before he slams into me, causing my back to arch and for me to cry out. It hurts, but it hurts so good. He grabs my legs behind my knees, pushing them back. With each thrust, I cry out. My headboard is smacking into the wall so hard I'm afraid we're going to put a hole in it, but I don't tell him to stop.

"You feel so fucking good, baby. So tight, so hot, and so fucking wet." He bends down and whispers against my lips. "Are you going to come again for me? Is my baby going to squeeze all the come out of my dick?"

My body spasms, and I begin to come...violently. My hands grip the top of his head as a scream rips from my throat.

"Oh fuck, baby. That's my girl." He begins to piston his hips, driving deeper and harder into me. My orgasm keeps going and going until his movements become erratic, and he finally plants

116

himself to the root, groaning against my neck.

"I think you killed me," I whisper against the top of his head, kissing his dark hair.

His chuckle vibrates against my chest, and he raises his head to smile down at me. "You look gorgeous for a dead girl." I whimper as he pulls out of me. "Let me get rid of this."

He gets up, and I admire his fantastic body as he walks naked across the hall to my bathroom. The toilet flushes, and then the sink turns on and off before he opens the door, walking back into my room. I unabashedly gawk at him as he comes toward the bed. His cock's still half hard, and he chuckles as he climbs into bed with me.

"Baby, you can't stare at my dick like that."

I smile up at him. "Like what?"

He smirks at me. "Like you want to devour my cock with that sweet mouth of yours."

Pulling the blankets over us, he pulls me until I'm lying half on and half off him, and his arms are wrapped tightly around me. "Hmmm…maybe later." My voice sounds sleepy.

Joe places his lips against my forehead. "Sleep, baby."

That's exactly what I do.

***

Joe places a steak on my plate and then does the same to his. We take them to my kitchen table, where I have two glasses of sweet tea waiting.

Today's been the best day ever. After we woke up the second time, he carried me into the shower.

We took turns washing each other in between kisses and caresses. After we were done, he fed my cats and made us coffee and toast while I got ready. Our plan was to ride around on his bike and do some sightseeing.

I braided my hair and just put a little mascara, powder, and lip gloss on. In my bedroom, I threw on cut-off jean shorts, a red sleeveless t-shirt, and my black Adidas. In my closet, I grabbed the jean jacket I was bringing to wear while we rode around.

After toast and coffee, we rode to his hotel so he could get changed. I got to meet his friends, and apparently he missed a big party in their suite because the place was littered with beer and liquor bottles.

I'm no prude, but a girl in just panties came out of one of the bedrooms while I was waiting for Joe to change. Joe's friend Chris was asking me about my band and where we played. He was nice enough, but he kept staring at my tits. I was saved, though, when Joe exited the bathroom, grabbed my hand, and shouted bye to his friends as we left.

"Chris was staring at your chest, wasn't he?" His voice was slightly growly, which kind of surprised me and turned me on.

"Um...yeah, he was." Joe shook his head. "It's okay. Unfortunately, it happens."

Once we were on the elevator, he pulled me to him, attacking my lips with vigor. My tongue reached for his in a duel that had me tingling all over. As soon as we reached the lobby and the doors dinged, Joe pulled me out of the elevator and out into the warm, humid air. The smell of the damp grass tickled my nose as we walked toward the parking lot to his bike.

After I climbed on behind him, my arms wrapped around his waist. Again, my hands rested on his hard abs, making it hard to concentrate, especially since I knew what those abs looked like while he fucked me.

I cleared those thoughts, and we made it to our first destination: the zoo. I've always loved going there. I felt like an excited child as we moved from exhibit to exhibit. We took pictures of each other and selfies. At one point, Joe carried me around the park piggyback.

When I had refused to go into the reptile exhibit, he'd picked me up and carried me in there screaming. Finally, the staff came over and asked us to leave the exhibit. "Oh my God, I could kill you!" I had screeched.

Then, of course, Joe felt bad because he had no idea that I was deathly afraid of snakes. When I was little, I had found a copperhead in the backyard, and it had chased me until my pops killed it with a shovel. They said my scream had taken years off both their lives. It took a long time before I'd even go in the backyard.

Thankfully that didn't put a damper on our day. We ended our time at the zoo with the train ride. I had laid my head on his shoulder feeling content and happy—happier than I've felt since I lost the baby. I began to push the thought away, but I couldn't help but imagine a little dark-haired, blue-eyed beauty sitting on her daddy's lap, smiling as we rode the train as a little family.

It was like Joe knew where my thoughts had gone, because he sighed as he kissed my forehead.

After we left, we rode around for a little bit and then went back to my place to get my car to go to the grocery store and buy steaks and all the fixin's.

Which brings me back to now. "What time are you heading back tomorrow?" The thought of him leaving makes me sad. I've enjoyed spending time with him.

"The plan is to be on the road at ten." He takes a drink of his tea and then looks at me. "Is it weird that I don't want to leave you?"

Shaking my head, I get out of my chair and move around toward him. Joe's eyes darken as he scoots his chair back. I reach him and place both hands on his shoulders before straddling his lap. I lean forward until our lips are almost touching. "It's not weird," I whisper right before my lips are on his.

***

I grab onto the headboard as I begin to bounce up and down harder while impaled on Joe's hard cock. I feel my orgasm build slowly. Joe's fingers pluck at my nipples, alternately sucking a tip into his mouth. His other hand reaches between us, strumming my clit with his thumb.

"Chloe, I want to hear you come. It's fucking music to my ears." My neck arches back as he pinches my clit, sending me into oblivion. His hips buck up, and he pulls me down as he groans against my neck. He wraps his arms around me and falls to his back. The only sound to be heard is our matching, panting breaths.

My lips press against his rapidly beating pulse. "What a way to say goodbye." His chuckle is deep and a balm to my soul. Joe squeezes me before rolling us. I whimper as he pulls out of me.

"I'll be right back." I roll to my side, tucking my hands under my pillow. My cats both come trotting in and jump on the bed, giving me stern "Meows." Joe comes back in, and Ragnar gives him the stink eye, especially when he climbs back in bed and pulls me against his chest. He leans over me and reaches for Ragnar, scratching him behind his ear. "She wanted it, dude." I giggle as he talks to my cat.

Ragnar answers. "*Meow.*"

"I don't think that helped your case."

He kisses my bare shoulder. "Yeah, I'm getting that." Joe pulls me close. "I really should get up so I can get showered and back to the hotel."

I reach out and snag my phone off the nightstand to check the time. It's eight thirty. "Why don't you shower and I'll make some coffee and a quick breakfast?"

He pushes me down on my back, settling between my legs. "That sounds good." Joe kisses my lips slowly. I watch as he climbs out of bed, not missing the massive erection he has. Licking my lips, I watch as he picks his clothes up. "Baby, stop looking at me like that."

"Sorry, I was just enjoying the view." I climb out of bed and slip my robe on before making my way toward the kitchen. I hear the shower kick on, and I quickly start a pot of coffee.

By the time Joe comes walking into the kitchen with no shirt on, I'm plating our scrambled eggs and toast. We sit side by side while we eat. Laggie and Ragnar both sit by my feet, upset that I'm not giving them my undivided attention.

When we finish, I want to wrap myself around Joe so he can't leave, but I know that's irrational, and he has a life to get back to. Is this it for us? The moment he steps out of my house, am I going to be forgotten?

I shake off those thoughts as I walk with him to my front door. He brushes my hair back from my face and places his lips tenderly on my forehead. "I'll call you or text you when I get home."

"Oh, you don't have to do that. You're going to be tired."

He raises a brow at me. "I know I don't have to, but I want to." Joe places his lips on mine. The kiss is chaste compared to the others we've shared but no less enjoyable. "I had an amazing weekend. I'm going to miss you."

"I'm going to miss you, too. Be safe." He kisses me one more time—this kiss is all tongues, teeth, and hair grabbing. When he pulls back, I can't help but whimper. "Go before I don't let you leave."

I watch him walk to his bike and climb on. The rumble of the bike sends a tingle through me, but then a lump forms in my throat as I watch him give me a chin lift and then take off down my street.

In the kitchen, I place my fingers to my lips because they're still tingling. I begin to clean up the kitchen while I drink my cup of coffee. It doesn't make sense—why do I feel sad? We barely know each other, he's seven years younger than me, and we live four hours away from each other. A relationship between us wouldn't work…right?

Chapter Ten

Joe

My feet pound the asphalt of the track at my high school as I run lap after lap. I got home a little after six last night, and I was so exhausted that I just shot Chloe a quick text and then crashed.

This morning, I woke up hard as a rock and had to jerk off. I called her after I was done, and she was still lying in bed, which made my dick hard again. I love hearing Chloe's voice all sleepy, sexy, and hoarse.

"How was your ride home?"

"It was good but long. I was tired and crashed as soon as I texted you. I just got up and just really fucking missed you. Is Ragnar glad I'm gone?" Her sleepy giggle was really adorable.

"Of course. He's been doing cartwheels since you left. If I say your name, he hisses and sticks his claws out like Wolverine."

I started laughing and shook my head because she's so fucking cute. "What's on your agenda today?"

"I'm going to work on some pieces that need to be finished then have dinner at my parents' house." Her voice got quiet. "They've been kind of worried about me."

"They love you. Of course they're going to be worried. We didn't talk about it much."

"I know, and actually I'm kind of grateful that we didn't. We said what needed to be said, and I'm just thankful that you forgive me for what I said."

"Of course I forgive you. You forgave me too, you know."

Her sigh echoed through the phone. "We really screwed things up in the beginning, didn't we?"

"Yeah, but now we have the chance to start fresh." *Fuck*, I hoped that was what she wanted too.

"Really? How can this work? We live too far away."

I obviously hadn't thought about the logistics yet. "We'll take it a week at a time. Chloe, I feel like there's something here worth exploring. Please tell me that you feel it too."

"I do. It's just going to be different. Joe, if we do this, please don't sleep with anyone else. I know I don't have the right—"

"Of course you have the right. I know you've heard unflattering things about me from my aunt and uncle, and maybe some of it's true, but I'm not a cheater. Every relationship I've had—it hasn't been many—I've been faithful…always."

"It wasn't from Tay Tay or Dustin. It was your sister and cousins. They used to make comments here and there, but they were never terrible. Just that you liked the ladies and the ladies liked you." She sighed into the phone. "I haven't had the best luck in relationships. When I was younger, it was because I had two dads so I must've been molested or abused.

"Then it was curiosity, and they just wanted to see if they…I don't know…dressed like women, listened to show tunes all of the time, and whatever other misconception they could come up with. As I got older and being gay didn't have the same stigma attached to it, it got easier, but when you choose the wrong person, it makes a difference, and I just haven't been able to pick the right ones."

"Chloe, I don't know what's going to happen, and I can't guarantee that we won't hurt each other, but I will not cheat on you. And if I don't feel it's working anymore, I'll tell you. I just expect the same."

I hung up shortly after that with plans to talk the next night, which brings me to now.

After several laps around the track, I stop by the benches and grab my bottle of water, taking a huge swig. I pick up my phone and see I have a voicemail. After punching in my security code, my messages start playing.

"It's Mom. Just want to check if you're coming for dinner tonight. Your sister and the kids are coming. Call me back. I love you."

I hit her number and put it back to my ear. "Hi, honey," she says. "How was your weekend?"

Oh what to tell, what not to tell. "It was good. I…I saw Chloe."

"You did? How—how is she? I've wanted to call

126

her, but I didn't know if it was appropriate or not. I mean, that was my grandbaby, and I just hurt for her, you know?" My mom is by far the sweetest woman in the world.

"She's doing better. I think she'd like it if you called her. I'll text you her number. What time should I be over?"

"Six. Your brother will be here. It'll be so nice to have all my babies and grandbabies under one roof." My mom loves the chaos, and my niece and nephews eat up the attention they get from their gigi. "We're going to do burgers and hot dogs."

"Do you need me to bring anything?"

"Just yourself." We hang up a moment later. I grab my water bottle and start making my way toward my car.

Once I get home, I shower then throw on some basketball shorts and a sleeveless t-shirt. In the living room, I lie down on the couch to take a quick nap. It was a long but phenomenal weekend.

***

I step inside my childhood home and hear screaming coming from the back. Moving through the house, I see everyone is outside, and I step out of the back door. Parker has Natalie on his back, and he's chasing the boys.

"Hey, guys." Abby comes over with her cute belly, and a wave of sadness washes over me. I try to hide it, but she doesn't miss it. She places a hand on her stomach, and tears run down her cheeks.

"I'm sorry, Joe." She wraps her arms around my

middle. "The kids and I can go."

I know a lot of this is hormones. "No, I don't want you to go. It's just a shit thing that happened. I'm so happy for you and for Ben. No one deserves this more than you. I'll have another little niece to spoil."

She smiles up at me. "I love you, baby brother."

"I love you, big sister." Abby disappears inside the house. I spot my mom and dad giving me the same look. "I'm fine." Walking up to them, I wrap my arm around my mom's shoulders. "Abby's just hormonal, and getting upset isn't going to change anything. It's also not going to stop me from being happy for her or for Vi. Life goes on." I take a deep breath and hope they believe this nonchalant attitude.

Little arms wrap around my leg, and I pick up my nephew Dalton. "Unka Joe pway wiff me."

He's the perfect distraction. I throw him over my shoulder and carry him down the steps and toward my brother, who is chasing Natalie with Rion in his arms. "Should we get Uncle Parker?"

"Yes!" We charge after them, and they all start running and screaming. Haddie comes running down the stairs and snags Rion from Parker, and we all start chasing each other. My nephews and niece's laughter is music to my ears.

Abby calls for the kids so they can get washed up before dinner. She always handles all three of them with quick efficiency, with or without Ben's help. Haddie follows behind them—no doubt to help with the crew.

Parker sets the table while I set up the high chair

for Rion and strap Dalton's booster seat to his chair. It's loud, crazy, and chaotic, but my mom and dad don't stop smiling. Natalie is snuggled up to her pawpaw, telling him some story, and he's just eating it up. Mom doesn't let Abby make the kids' plates because she loves taking care of her grandbabies, and that's what she does while we make up our plates. Abby used to fight her about it but finally gave up. My mom is like a mama Grizzly bear, especially with the little ones.

Conversation is next to impossible while we eat—the kids all vie for their grandparents' attention while shoveling food into their sweet faces. Images assail me of a raven-haired, blue-eyed little girl sitting amongst her cousins, and my stomach turns.

I excuse myself, and in the bathroom I splash cold water on my face. I sit on the closed toilet and pull out my phone.

Joe: Hey you.

Chloe: Hi! How was dinner at your parents' house?

Joe: I'm still here. Just hiding in the bathroom.

Chloe: Why? Are you okay?

Joe: Yes…No…My sister and her kids are here and I just thought about our baby and I…I don't know I'm just all over the place. Sorry.

She doesn't answer me right away, and I think maybe it was wrong to bring it up, but then my notifications go off.

Chloe: Don't be sorry. If it helps, it does get easier. Violet called me earlier and I knew she was happy about her baby but scared to share that, but life goes on and I would never begrudge her for being happy.

It's good to know that we're on the same wavelength.

Joe: My sister cried earlier because she felt guilty too. I told my parents the same thing. My mom asked if it would be okay if she called you.

Chloe: Of course she can. That's really sweet of her, I've always loved JoJo.

I smile because she's using my mom's nickname.

Joe: I guess I should head back out there. Can I call you when I get home?

Chloe: Yeah I'd like that.

Joe: Great, I'll talk to you later.

Standing up, I tuck my phone into my pocket and splash some more cold water on my face. When I open the door, I'm surprised to find my brother standing with his back against the opposite wall.

"What's up?"

"Can we talk for a minute?"

I follow him out the front door onto the porch. "Everything okay?"

"Yeah. We just haven't had a chance to talk, and I wanted to tell you how sorry I am."

I grab him and pull him into a hug. I've never shied away from showing affection to anyone in my family. "Thanks, Park. Did they say anything when I got up?"

"No, they looked concerned, but I told them I'd check on you." He leans in close to me. "Chloe's fucking hot. Way to go, man."

I just shake my head at my brother, and I can honestly say that I don't like him thinking about Chloe that way. "Watch it, little brother." I give him a playful shove.

His eyes widen comically. "Is my brother seriously into this woman? I think so." Parker shoves me back. "Oh, how the mighty have fallen."

Have I fallen? Maybe…I don't know, but I definitely want to see where it goes with us. Of course, the odds are stacked against us; she's seven years older, we live four hours apart, and maybe all she wants from me is a fling—no, she said she felt it too, but what if she just said that because I did?

No, Chloe is not the type to play games. Even when she was still pregnant, she was honest with me about everything.

"Shut the fuck up. I haven't fallen, but we're going to see where it goes, and maybe it'll become something more than what it is right now. How's

Charleston?"

"Fucking great. Uncle Cash redid the basement, so I've got a little apartment down there so I can have privacy. Of course I don't bring girls home, but if I don't come home at night, I don't get any grief."

Our nephew Rion chooses that moment to come to the screen door screaming, "Unc, Unc!" I open the door and grab him, lifting him into my arms. He screeches and then slaps my cheeks before giving me a sloppy kiss. Then the little man lunges for Parker, who gets the same treatment.

After that, we head back inside, and I finish my dinner while Mom and Abby start serving dessert. My mom sets mine in front of me, kisses the side of my head, and whispers, "I love you, honey."

"Love you too."

My mom sends Parker and me home with leftovers, and Haddie and I make plans to meet for lunch. I help Abby get the kids strapped into their car seats and promise Natalie that I'll come over for a playdate soon.

After they leave, Parker and I sit out back with Dad and have a beer. He stares out across our backyard, and I can't help but wonder what's on his mind. Parker looks at me with a raised brow, and all I can do is shrug.

Finally, he turns around and sits across from us. "I'm so proud of you boys and the men you're becoming. I know you both have been wild. Don't think I don't hear the stories about you both. I was the same way until I met your mom and she changed everything." He looks at me. "If you feel like there's something worth fighting for in Chloe, then you fucking fight for her." *What's happening?* He then turns to Parker. "You…make sure you're safe."

After our dad hugs us, he heads inside. Parker turns to me. "Is Dad dying or something?"

I shake my head. "No, maybe it's Chloe losing the baby and Abby being pregnant again. We're all growing up. Maybe it's just freaking him out."

"Yeah, maybe you're right. I'm heading in. I have to be up early to drive back to Charleston in the morning, and Mom promised homemade biscuits and gravy if I stayed." He disappears inside. I swallow the rest of my beer and take the empty bottle inside before saying goodbye to my folks.

Haddie left a while ago to meet someone—she just wouldn't say who. I hate that my baby sister is a knockout. I haven't missed the way guys look at her. It makes me borderline homicidal because I'm a guy who knows exactly what is going through their minds. I have half a mind to go track her ass down and see who she's meeting, but I won't. She's eighteen and able to make her own decisions…I guess.

My mom walks me out when I take my leave. "Is Dad okay? He was getting deep with Parker and me outside earlier, and it kind of freaked us out."

"Oh, he's fine. We were with your aunts and uncles the other day for lunch, and we just got to talking about all you kids and how great everyone is doing. I think it just hit us how blessed we are." She grabs my arm and gives it a squeeze. "Don't get me wrong—you've all put us through the ringer at some point, but you've all found your paths, and we're grateful for that."

I kiss her cheek and promise to come by for dinner one night this coming week.

Chapter Eleven

Chloe

I'm just putting the finishing touches on a bracelet when my phone rings. I get that familiar warm, tingly feeling in my belly when Joe's name pops up on my screen. Over the past week, this is what our relationship, if that's what this is, has entailed: long phone calls or texting back and forth for hours.

Things have gotten better this past week. I feel great physically, and I'm getting there mentally and emotionally. I've been dodging Reggie and Elizabeth's calls because I just don't want to deal with them. I'm still really hurt that my trust was betrayed like it was. Hailey has been super nice, but I'm figuring it's the guilt talking…maybe. I've kept things with us professionally pleasant.

She doesn't know how I found out, and she hasn't brought it up, so why should I? She'd probably just run back to her sister anyway. My parents have finally stopped hovering and looking at me with those sad looks. Of course it's because I finally had to sit them both down and state it very clearly that I was okay.

I answer the phone and put it on speaker so I can work and talk. "Hey, you. How's it going?"

"I fucking miss you." I love when his voice gets growly. He can't see the huge smile on my face.

"I miss you, too. Are you working right now?"

"No, I just got home. It was a long fucking day. I think I'm going to shower and head to bed soon. What are you doing?"

"Working on a bracelet, and then I was going to pour myself a glass of wine and watch *iZombie*."

My doorbell chimes, and I get up, moving through the house. "Joe, are you still there?" I look through the window and can't help the big smile on my face. Ripping the door open, I can't help but squeal. "What are you doing here? I thought you were just getting home from work."

"Are you going to let me in?" I push open the screen door and jump into Joe's arms. "I take it you're happy to see me."

"Yes, so happy." He carries me into the house while I continue to smile at him. "What are doing here? I thought you worked today."

"I was supposed to, but I switched with someone and wanted to surprise you. I hope that was okay." He starts to look unsure of himself even though I'm in his arms.

"Of course it's okay. I do have a little gig tonight."

"A little one?"

I smile at him. "It's little because it's just me and

the piano."

"Is it okay if I come watch?" It gives me a little thrill that he wants to come watch me.

I kiss his forehead. "Of course you can. Just FYI: my parents, Carter, and Eli will be there."

I don't miss the way he slightly cringes at my words. "Hey, I promise they'll behave. It sucks sometimes being the only female. They're all protective of me."

He reaches up and tucks a loose strand of hair behind my ear. "I can see why they would be. It'll be fine. Show me what you were working on?"

Unfortunately, he sets me down. Grabbing his hand, I lead him to my spare bedroom that's part workshop, part music room. He gazes around the room—I'm sure taking in the pictures of me in musicals, talent shows, and pageants when I was younger. I don't keep them up because I'm vain or anything but just to remind me of a fun time in my life.

"God, you were beautiful back then, too."

How can this man make me blush? "Thank you. You can sit in here and hang out with me if you want. I just need to finish this bracelet. It's for Eli's mom." I sit back down on my stool. "Help yourself to something to drink. You can sit in here with me or watch TV in the living room if you want."

He kisses the top of my head before disappearing. I stick my earbuds in and turn on some working music—Classical. A minute later, I feel him reenter the room and sit down next to me. My fingers work quickly to add the last of the gemstones, and then I tie off the end and attach the clasp.

Now that it's finished, I spray it with a gentle cleanser to get all my fingerprints off. Once it's all polished, I place it in a little box and then tie it with my signature lavender ribbon.

I clean up my space. Joe heads out in the living room, and when I enter, I find him sitting on the sofa watching baseball. I move around and sit down next to him. He wraps his arm around my shoulders. "I'm really glad you're here." I smile up at him, and he leans down, kissing my forehead.

"I'm glad. I almost turned around twice because I didn't want to seem like a creepy stalker, but I just wanted to see you. Do you want to go have dinner before you play tonight?"

"Sure. What were you thinking?"

"Last time I was up here, I saw a steakhouse by the hotel. It's called Vaughn's. Have you been there?"

"I don't think I have, but that sounds great."

He gives my shoulder a squeeze. "I know it might be presumptuous, but I brought an overnight bag. I'm going to get it, okay?"

I smile at him. "Yes, of course." He gets up and runs outside to grab it. While he's outside, his phone chirps. My eyes drift toward it and see a text alert from someone named Shaya. *Ugh, why did I look? It's not my business.* He said he wasn't going to sleep with anyone while whatever this is was happening, and I need to trust that and him.

Joe steps back in with his bag slung over his shoulder. "I'm going to stick this in your bedroom."

While he does that, my mind keeps going back to

his phone and this Shaya girl. Who is she?…No, I'm not going to be that girl. He's not Trevor.

Trevor Phillips had been the love of my life, or so I thought. We were together for five years, and I thought he was the one until I learned that I wasn't his only girlfriend and one was pregnant. I swear it turned into an episode of *Maury*.

A smile touches my lips when I remember the way he showed up at the apartment we'd shared to get his stuff. Trevor had called me a slut, and my pops punched him right in the face. Last I heard, he's still single, has two kids by two different women, and pays a ton in child support.

Then there was the Teddy debacle, but when I look back, that was more of a rebound, and it was the catalyst that had me seeking Joe out.

Yes, both of those guys have given me a little bit of trust issues, and it's made me a little more selective. Joe isn't the usual type I'd go for. He's charismatic and gorgeous, and women look at him like he's a meal. I know his reputation, but can I trust that he'll be faithful with me?

"What time do you have to be at your gig tonight?" He sits back down, wrapping his arm around my shoulders.

"I have to be there at eight thirty, and I go on at nine. We should probably go to dinner at six or so—unless that's too early, of course."

"Not at all." He picks up his phone. I watch as he pulls up Shaya's text and then deletes it.

"Everything okay?" What am I doing? I cringe and wish I kept silent.

He looks at me, giving me a smile. "Yeah, just

an old hookup checking in." Joe turns fully toward me. "I meant what I said. While this—whatever this is—is going on, there won't be anyone else.

"Before you, there have been other women...I won't lie, and I'm not ashamed. I've never lied to any of them. They all knew I wasn't looking for anything serious. I've also never treated any of them poorly. If that's going to be a problem, tell me now and we can end things. If it's not, then let's get ready to go out to a fantastic dinner, and then I can watch you play later."

"Thank you for that. I appreciate your honesty. I dated a guy for five years—actually, we lived together, and he had this whole secret life and even had a baby on the way while we were together. It's made me slightly paranoid. You'll have to bear with me." Joe grabs a strand of my hair and pulls me to him.

Our lips meet in a slow, sensual glide. Our tongues meet and duel—I moan as he deepens the kiss. Pushing up onto my knees, I lean into him, gripping his shirt in my fists. I feel one of his hands slide into my hair, grabbing it at the base of my skull. I whimper from the bite of pain as he gives it a jerk and nips at my bottom lip.

Joe might be only twenty-four, but he's got the bedroom skills of a much older, more experienced man. He pulls away first, and I really want to pout. "I wasn't done with you yet," I murmur against his lips.

"I know, but if we don't stop, we won't make dinner and you won't make your show. Why don't you get ready? I just need to change my clothes."

He's right, and I do need to get ready. I've already showered, so I just have to do my hair and makeup and then get dressed. "Okay, you can get ready in my room. I'll be in the bathroom." I kiss him before getting up and heading into the bathroom.

It doesn't take long for me to do my face. I give my eyelids a smoky look that makes the blue pop and add a little color to my cheeks to give them a dewy look. I decide to use a popping red on my lips.

My ebony locks hang in smooth waves down my back. The front is twisted and pinned back from my face, showing off the diamond stud earrings my grandma bought me for my thirtieth birthday. They go with the matching solitaire that hangs around my neck.

The dress I chose for tonight is hanging on the back of the door. It's a royal blue capped sleeve midi dress that hits me right below my knees. It hugs my curves and makes me feel so sexy. I slip it on and smooth my hands over the material. After dabbing my face with a little powder, I stick it and my lipstick in my little bag.

After dabbing some perfume on, I open the bathroom door. I move across the hall to my bedroom and grab my black stiletto pumps, slipping them on before heading into the living room. Joe is standing in front of the TV, and it gives me a second to admire his sexy backside, which looks spectacular in his black dress pants. He turns as I walk farther into the room, and the look on his face makes my pussy tingle.

His eyes rake over my body, and it does an

involuntary shiver. He stalks toward me, and I automatically back up until I'm against the wall. Grabbing my wrists, he pulls my arms up over my head then shackles them with one hand. My breath leaves me in little pants as his other hand wraps around my throat.

Can he see my pulse pounding in my neck? Can he feel it? His heated gaze holds mine as his hand slides from my neck to my breasts. A gasp slips past my lips as his thumb grazes my nipple. "You are so fucking beautiful." His hand begins moving again, slowly down my stomach until he reaches the hem of my dress.

Joe leans forward until our lips are almost touching. I moan as I feel him lift my dress, his hand sliding up my bare thigh. His touch is firm, demanding. He reaches the apex of my thighs, and a sexy growl comes from his lips. It's because he's discovering I'm not wearing any panties.

Thank God I just got waxed last week. His fingers slide through my slick folds, and I moan. I think he's going to kiss me, but instead of touching my lips, he touches my chin and then my neck.

I want to touch him so bad, but he won't let go of me. My breasts feel heavy, my pussy aches to be filled, and I want his lips on mine. He works one finger inside me. My head hits the wall with a *thunk*, but I don't care.

Meow...Meow. Ragnar and Lagertha had been lounging in my room on my bed all day, and now they've decided to come out and visit. Joe pulls away from me, and we both look down. Both cats have gotten in between us and are staring at us. I start to laugh, and Joe joins in as we stare at these little monsters.

I look up at Joe. "They've been sleeping all day. I swear they are doing this just to be brats." He pulls his finger out of me and brings it to his lips, licking my juices off it. My eyes don't leave his mouth while he does it.

"Mmmm…" Joe moans around his finger. "You taste so fucking good."

"You're making me want to cancel my gig tonight and take you to bed." He lets go of my wrists, and I wind my arms around his neck. "I haven't had the chance yet to tell you how handsome you look." He gives me that cocky smirk, but I love it.

"Go ahead and tell me." I shake my head.

"You look so handsome." I playfully pinch his cheeks. I slide past him while he adjusts himself and go into the kitchen, where I get my babies a treat.

Joe comes into the kitchen. "We better leave now or we seriously won't leave."

I move toward him and run my hands over the white linen shirt he's wearing. His sleeves are rolled up to his forearms. It really is a crime to look as good as he does. My hand slides down and cups his dick, which is semi hard. "Poor baby." He growls as he moves toward me.

"No big boy. No more hanky panky. I promise when we get back tonight, I'll make it worth your while." I hold my hands up in a halting gesture.

"How will you make it worth my while?"

I lock up and let Joe lead me to his car. "You'll just have to wait and see."

Chapter Twelve

Joe

As the night wears on, I can barely control myself around her. I've never had such an amazing date. We've been clicking on all levels, and I know for a fact that this will be worth it. I just hope she feels the same.

Dinner at Vaughn's had been amazing. While she had been getting ready, I called and was able to get us a last-minute reservation. When we stepped inside, the maître d, who couldn't keep his fucking eyes off Chloe, led us to an intimate table in the corner. He tried to pull her chair out for her, but I gave him a look I hoped conveyed the fact that I didn't want him touching her or her chair.

She looked at me, and her cheeks turned an adorable shade of pink. Chloe ordered a glass of water, and I ordered a beer. She was going to wait until our meals came before she ordered some wine. "I can't get tipsy before I play." I could understand that.

"Did anything happen with you and that Hailey after what I told you?" It still pissed me off what happened to her. Women are far meaner than most guys I know.

She shrugged her shoulders. "She's been overly nice, but I'm sure it's her guilty conscience. Reggie and Elizabeth have been trying to reach out, but I'm not ready to talk to them yet. What they did, or what Elizabeth did, hurt me and broke my trust."

My hand slid across the table and covered hers. When will the pain of our loss stop? A part of me wants to put another baby inside of her, but she's not ready for that yet, and to be quite honest, I'm not ready either. But I will be, and the more I imagine my future, the more I see her there, and any children we'd be blessed to have.

My dad always told me that he knew right away that my mom was it for him—even though at first he got scared and ran. After they finally reunited, that was all she wrote. I was eighteen when I finally got the whole story about what happened with them and why he wasn't in any pictures until I was over a year old.

"You don't have to explain to me, babe. What they did was awful, but enough of that talk. How are your parents?" Both men hate me, but who could blame them? I left their daughter when she needed me most. At least her brother has been cool with me, but he seems to be cool with everyone.

"They're good. They've both been really busy with work lately, so I haven't seen a whole lot of them."

"What do they do?"

"My dad, Garrett, is an electrician and my dad, Ian, is a physical therapist. Your dad and Dustin own their own company, right?"

I watched her delicate fingers wrap around her glass. "Yeah, with my uncle Luke. My dad was slightly disappointed that I didn't go into the family business, but law enforcement is my passion. You know what happened to my sister, right?" Chloe nodded her head. "After that, I knew without a doubt that was what I wanted."

Chloe surprised me by reaching across the table and grabbing my hand. "It may be too soon to say this, but I worry about you. I know being an officer can be dangerous." She let go of my hand and covered her face. "Oh God. I probably sound like a freak show." Chloe peeked at me between her fingers, and I laughed softly.

"You don't sound like a freak show. It's sweet…really. It's just nice to know you're thinking about me when I'm not around."

Our waiter set our plates in front of us, and Chloe ordered a glass of wine before he left. "Maybe I am."

"Good, because I think about you all of the time." Our gazes stayed locked, my pulse pounded, and my dick was hard as a rock. She is so fucking beautiful, and I'm learning more and more that she's beautiful on the inside, too. "I can't wait to see you play again tonight."

"I'm excited for you to see me play." She cut into her steak and took a bite, moaning softly around the hunk of meat. I worked on my own, not because I was hungry but because I had to distract myself from the delicious little sounds she makes while she eats.

We finished eating our meals and declined dessert since we had to make our way toward the bar. She excused herself to go to the bathroom, and I didn't miss the appreciating eyes that were all following her as she moved through the restaurant. I couldn't blame them, but I gripped the table to keep myself from knocking each one of them out.

She came back, and I'd already paid the check, so I stood up and wrapped an arm around her waist as I led her out of the restaurant and to my car. "Thank you for dinner," she said.

I kissed her temple.

We pulled up and found a spot in the parking lot of Whiskey Bar and Lounge. It's just a nondescript brick building, nothing to write home about. The moment we walked inside, though, I was in awe— dark wood covers the floor, the tables and chairs are all black and smooth. The bar top is white and almost looks like granite. Bronzed sconces illuminate the room in a soft, romantic glow.

In the corner sits a beautiful black baby grand piano. Next to the piano is a set of French doors that open to a huge terrace that allows us to see downtown Atlanta illuminated.

Now that we're here, the place isn't packed, but it's full. With my arm around her waist, we weave our way through the tables and head toward the bar. My eyes scan the room as she talks to the older man behind the bar. I spot her family as they come walking in and move toward them. I don't miss the looks of surprise on their faces.

"Joe? What a surprise," her dad, Ian, says, offering his hand.

I take it and then reach out my hand to Garrett, who reluctantly shakes it. His eyes look thoughtful as he takes me in. "How are you doing, son?"

I don't miss the meaning behind his words. Leaning in, I murmur, "I'm better, but more so knowing that Chloe is healing."

His eyes glisten, and I'm worried the guy is going to start crying, but instead he gives me a smile. "She is, thankfully, and I'm glad it's getting better for you."

Carter stands off to the side, shaking his head and looking toward the ceiling. "Hey, Carter, how are you? Where's Eli? I'm surprised he's not lurking in the corner waiting to kick my ass."

"He had a date, but he said he'd try to make it. I'm good, though. You're in for a treat tonight. My sister is phenomenal."

Chloe joins us a moment later and greets her parents and brother before leading us to a reserved table by the French doors, and from there I'll have a prime view of her while she plays.

The waitress comes, and we order drinks. I try to hand her my credit card to start a tab, but her dad gets to her first. I still try to offer her mine, but he gives me a look that has me stuffing it back in my wallet.

I love watching Chloe with her family. It's clear they all adore her. I honestly believed that they were going to give me the cold shoulder, but they're including me.

They start asking me about my job when the

lights dim and Chloe comes out. She gracefully sits at the piano and pulls the microphone close to her. "Good evening. I'm Chloe, and I'll be playing for you tonight."

She talks to the crowd for a minute, and then she begins to play. Her brother was right—she *is* phenomenal. She was great the other time I saw her, but this time with just her and a piano, she's beautiful.

Chloe sings everything from Elton John to Lady Gaga. A couple older couples dance in the little space that I honestly wouldn't call a dance floor. I glance at her family, and the look on their faces is pure pride. Garrett pulls Ian into his side, kissing his temple.

She finishes her song, takes a drink of water, and starts talking. "How's everyone doing?" The crowd claps and whistles. "I'm going to sing one more song then take a little break. This is an emotional song, so just bear with me if I have trouble getting it out. It's called 'Stars' by Grace Potter and the Nocturnals."

Chloe's got me mesmerized as she sings. As I listen to the lyrics, I realize it's about our baby, or at least about that kind of loss. Throughout most of the song, her eyes are closed, the emotions flowing off her.

She's got the room captivated, and I can't blame them. When the song finally ends, she doesn't move from her bench. I begin to think I should grab her, but she finally stands up, giving a little curtsy as we all stand and applaud.

We stay standing as she comes over to us. I let

her dads and brother hug her first. When she comes to stand in front of me, I grab her face and kiss her lips firmly. I pull back. "That was beautiful, baby."

"Thank you."

I flag down the waitress and order Chloe a glass of wine and an ice water, and then we all relax until she has to go on again.

***

We step into Chloe's place and are greeted by Ragnar and Lagertha. Chloe squats down to pet both cats. "Hi, my babies," she croons.

I bend down, giving them both a scratch on the head. Chloe stands up and slips her heels off.

The rest of our night went great. She was a little quiet after she sang that song, but everyone seemed to give her the space she seemed to need. Right before her second set, she let me pull her out to the "dance floor" and slow danced with me.

"That song was beautiful. You're so talented." She blushed for me, but I didn't miss the fact that her eyes were shiny. "I'm so proud of you for putting yourself out there like that. Everyone could feel the emotions coming off of you."

She rested her head on my shoulder as we swayed to the music coming through the speakers. "The first time I heard it, I loved it, but then I listened to the lyrics and loved it even more."

"You've made me a fan, that's for sure." Fuck, it felt good holding her in my arms like that, her body pressed up against mine. Alarm bells went off in my head because I knew I was falling for her too fast, but like my dad had told me—if she was who I wanted, then I needed to fight for her.

After we danced, I led her back to the bathrooms, and while I waited for her in the hall, I pulled out my phone. I'd felt it vibrate multiple times in my pocket. Pulling it out, I see I have five text messages.

April: Hey Joe what are you doing? Call me.

Tiffany: Hey big boy want to have some fun tonight?

Chris: You need to come party with me! There are hot chicks everywhere. Call me!

Jessica: Hey you! Guess who I'm sitting with??? Chris is here. Where are you?

Chris: Get here now! Jessica is looking smokin' hot tonight and she is wanting your dick.

I deleted each one. I'm not ashamed of my past, but those messages don't make me sound like a very good guy. What could I say? I've always loved sex and have a pretty high sex drive. My looks make it very easy to find willing bed partners. I've never lied or gave a woman false hope to get them into bed, and I've always been upfront about my intentions.

Some think they can win your heart with their magical pussy, but most just want the same thing—

a good time with no strings. Not since Tracey had I wanted someone else. Chloe stepped out of the bathroom, and I moved toward her. Her lips tipped up into a smile, and I began kissing her softly.

Reluctantly, I pulled away from her. I used my thumb to wipe off the lipstick I smudged. I led her back out to our table.

She sang for another half hour before finishing up. People flocked to her, praising her singing. Standing back with her family, I watched as she graciously talked to each person. Her smile was blinding and genuine, and she was really in her element.

We left a short time after that. Her parents walked us out, both hugging and kissing their daughter goodbye.

Now, I watch her stand up straight and lead her cats into the kitchen—I don't miss the provocative sway of her hips. I lock the front door and then follow her. She smiles at me when I step into the kitchen. I don't say anything; my eyes just follow her as she moves toward me.

Chloe places both hands on my chest and looks up at me. "Thank you for coming tonight—I loved knowing that you were sitting there watching me."

My fingers make their way into her hair. I grab it in my fists and yank her head back. Her pupils dilate, and her skin flushes. I bend down and lick her lips—she tries to reach for me with her mouth, but I don't let her move. The whimper that escapes her lips is turning me the fuck on.

I move her until her back is against the wall, caging her in. Shackling her wrists above her head with one hand, I reach down with the other and very slowly move my calloused hand up her silky smooth thigh. The whole time my eyes never leave hers. I don't miss the way her carotid beats rapidly in her neck.

I reach her pussy, not missing the wetness there and loving the sexy gasp that leaves her lips. I hit her clit, and she moans.

Chloe tries pulling her hands out of my grasp, but I hold tight. "Unh-unh, baby—I want to play, and you're going to let me." Her scent makes my cock even harder, and it's ready to punch a hole through my pants. "Mmmm…you smell delicious. I need to taste you. Spread your legs for me."

Chloe's dress is around her upper thighs so it's easy for her to spread them. I drop to my knees right there in her kitchen. I spread her lips with my thumbs before dragging my tongue through her damp folds. She moans loudly as I suck her clit between my lips and push a finger inside of her.

She is soaked and so fucking hot right now. Her pussy is trying to suck my finger in deeper as she convulses around it. I begin licking her pussy with vigor, loving the sound of her cries as I push her closer and closer to orgasm. She's so wet that her juices are running down the palm of my hand as I finger fuck her.

Chloe babbles and cries incoherently as I suck her clit between my lips and suck…hard.

"Oh God!" she cries as her pussy squeezes the fuck out of my finger.

Her orgasm begins to ebb, and she sags against the wall. I stand up. "Climb up, baby." She wraps her arms around my shoulders, and I put my hands on her ass as she jumps up. Chloe wraps her legs around my waist, her heels digging into my back, and it's making me hard as fuck.

I carry her through her house and set her on her feet. Her cats are on her bed, so I grab them and set them both outside. "I'm about to defile your mother." They both look unimpressed as I shut the door in their furry faces.

Chloe laughs softly as I walk toward her. "Did you just tell my cats that you were going to defile me?" While I was doing that, she'd stripped out of her dress and bra, leaving her in her sexy heels.

I can't speak—all I can do is nod before stalking toward her and tossing her on her bed. She bends her knees and spreads her legs, and I watch as she reaches between her legs and begins rubbing her clit.

"Fuck me, you're sexy." I rip my shirt off and quickly rip off my pants. I squeeze the tip of my cock to ease the ache, but it doesn't help. Climbing onto the bed, I feel like a predator stalking its prey. "Move your hand, Chloe." Her eyes widen, and she bites her lip. Slowly, she shakes her head. "Are you telling me no?"

"Maybe," she whispers softly. Her fingers slowly strum her clit.

"You're a bad girl." I grab her and flip her over so she's on all fours. "Cheek to the bed, baby." Chloe gets into position, and I groan because she's a fucking sight. My hand gently moves from her upper back down to her juicy ass. I raise my hand and bring it down on the fleshy globe.

She cries out and tries to cover her ass, but I grab her hands and pin them down. "Did you just spank me! You let me go right now, asshole." I let go and swat her again and then immediately slide my fingers through her sweet honey. Her moan is music to my ears. I swat her again twice in rapid succession and then dip my fingers into her pussy.

I can't wait anymore. I flip her to her back, then reach into her nightstand drawer to grab a condom. A groan slips past my lips as she wraps her hand around my aching cock. She lets go for me to slip the condom on.

"Spread your legs wider for me, baby." She does what I say, and I see her folds, glistening and hungry for my cock. "Fucking beautiful. Keep your legs just like that."

I grab her behind her thighs, opening her just a little bit more and then lining my cock up with her entrance. I push inside her excruciatingly slow, letting her feel every inch of me. When I'm finally buried to the hilt, we both groan. "God, you feel good."

She grabs my face, pulling it down and attacking my lips with hers. She's by far the best kisser I've had. I begin to move slowly in and out of her. She cries into my mouth as my thrusts begin to pick up pace.

I pull out of her and flip her back over to her hands and knees. I grab her hips right before I thrust inside her again, wrapping my arm around her chest and pulling her up to her knees. Her head flies back, and her hands clutch her headboard.

I fuck her hard, holding her tits in both of my

hands for leverage. "Give me your mouth." She turns, and I begin kissing her as I move. She wraps one arm around my neck, cupping the back of my head as we fuck.

I'm close to coming so I move one hand down between her legs, strumming her clit. Chloe pulls her mouth away and cries out. My thrusts become more violent as I feel her pussy ripple around me. "That's it, Chloe. Let me hear you come." Her mouth opens, and what sounds like a wail leaves her. She squeezes my dick so hard I have no choice but to follow her over the edge.

When I'm finally spent, I kiss the side of Chloe's head, smiling when she sags back against me. "You can spank me whenever you want," she says with a sigh.

I pull out of her, and we both collapse on her bed. Luckily, she has a wastebasket in her room, so I remove the condom, wrap it in a tissue, and throw it out. Chloe is lying on her side watching me; I reach out and brush her hair out of her face. "I didn't spank you too hard?"

"No. I honestly never thought I would like it, but I did…a lot. Maybe we could try other stuff, too." She leans into me, burrowing into the spot under my chin. I wrap my arms tightly around her and snuggle her close.

"Absolutely." I can't wait to do lots of stuff with her.

It's not long after that we both drift off into dreamland.

Chapter Thirteen

Chloe

I walk into the coffee shop by work and get in line. It's been two weeks since Joe surprised me, and I freaking miss him. Our dates over the two weeks have been phone calls, texts, and video chats. Sometimes we'll Facetime and just watch TV together. One time he watched me put together a bracelet.

While he was at his parents for dinner, he Facetimed me, and I got to say hi to his mom and dad, his brother and sisters, and of course his niece and nephews. They're so adorable, and I loved watching Joe with them. Of course I'd never say that it made me a little sad because he would've been a great father to our baby.

Last week, Violet texted me, checking in to see how I was doing. Per my request, she sent me a picture of her and her baby belly. She was positively glowing, and her husband is way hot—they looked so happy. Then she shocked the shit out

157

of me.

> *Violet: I have something I'm going to email you, but you can't tell Joe. He'd kill me if he found out.*

> *Chloe: What is it? You're scaring me?*

> *Violet: Oh it's nothing bad. Five years ago during a dance recital we did a special dance for our grandma and well…Just watch the video ☺*

I grabbed my laptop and opened my email. Violet's email was at the top, and I opened it, clicking on the video link. Tay Tay appears on the stage and introduces the grandkids. "Uptown Funk" plays, and I watch Daisy and Haddie dance around the stage. Then Cari, Lilah, and Abby come out and immediately start dancing.

The big finish comes up, and Violet and…*Oh my God, it's Joe.* He and Violet tap dance around the stage, and then they're joined by everyone else. I couldn't believe how good he was and was in awe of the way he could look so light on his feet considering how big he is. I closed the lid to my laptop and picked up my phone.

> *Chloe: OH…MY…GOD!!! I know he's your cousin, but he's so hot and he can dance.*

> *Violet: I knew you'd love it. He's a natural dancer, but he's always been too cool to do it.*

*I'm serious though don't tell him you saw that.
He tried to destroy all evidence, but I couldn't
let that happen* ☺

*Chloe: I promise I'll never let Joe know I saw
it. Love you girlie!*

*Violet: Love you too. Kiss everyone there for
me.*

I would never tell Violet that I watched his part
multiple times later that night and made sure to save
it under a fake title.

Work has been great. Hailey's been on vacation,
so I haven't had to deal with her. I've designed one
engagement ring and have another that I'll be
starting next week. I reach the counter and order my
skinny vanilla latte. My phone dings while I wait
for my drink.

It's a text from Joe.

*Joe: I just wanted to tell you good morning, I
miss you and I can't stop thinking about you.*

A fluttering feeling begins in my belly, and I
can't help but smile, but that's no different than any
other time he calls, messages, or whatever. I'm
falling in love with him, and I'm terrified. The odds
are not in our favor, but I can't stop even if we
should. I keep waiting for him to break things off
for someone his age, but he seems to be into this
whole hog.

Chloe: Good morning, I miss you too and I'm ALWAYS thinking about you.

Joe: Next weekend do you think you could come down here? My mom wants to have you over for dinner and a buddy of mine is having a party and I want you to meet some of my friends.

Chloe: I think I could swing that. This is a good time of year for me to do stuff on the weekends. Carter has a lot going on with his marching band so his weekends tend to be too busy to book any gigs.

Joe: Perfect. I can't wait to fucking see you. I have to get to work but I'll talk to you later.

Chloe: Be safe <3 <3

My name is called, and I thank them as I grab my drink. As I head toward the door, I hear my name being called. It's Elizabeth...fucking great. I don't really want to deal with this right now, especially before I head to work.

"Hey, Elizabeth, how are you?" I can be polite even if I want to kick something or someone.

"I'm good, but I've been worried about you. I want to explain something. I never told my sister what you said—she overheard me tell Reggie what progress I thought you were making, and she twisted it around. I would never betray your trust like that. I'm sad that you think I would, but I can understand why you'd think that.

"Chloe, Hailey's in rehab. She's not on vacation. We've been desperate for her to get help for a while. I hope you'll consider coming back to the group."

Wow, I wasn't expecting that, and it makes me sad that Hailey was battling demons and I had no clue. "Thank you for telling me that. I really hope she's getting the help she needs, and I'll think about coming back."

"Thank you, and I hope I see you soon." I watch her walk out of the coffee shop and can only shake my head and then head to work.

Later, I pull up in front of my parents' home and climb out of my car. As I step onto the front stoop, my dad opens the door. "Hi, honey. This is a nice surprise." I walk to him and wrap my arms around his waist. "Chloe, are you okay?"

With my cheek resting against his chest, I whisper, "I'm falling in love with him, and I'm terrified."

I feel him touch his lips to the top of my head. "Come inside—your pops bought that ice cream you like."

He leads me inside and gets me situated at the breakfast bar. He's silent while he dishes us up bowls of ice cream and then sets down a bowl in front of me before taking his seat. He's the one who was there for me the most when I found out the extent of what Trevor had done.

"Why are you scared? Things are going well, aren't they?" He's started warming up to Joe more than Pops has.

"Yeah, they are. I guess I'm just worried because he's a lot younger, and what if he decides I'm too old for him?"

My dad throws his head back and laughs. "Honey, you act like there's a huge age difference. What is there—a four-, five-year difference?" I hold up seven fingers. "Sweetheart, seven years in the grand scheme of things is nothing. Does he say it's a problem?" I shake my head. "Okay, then have you told him how you feel?"

"No, because I'm not sure where his head is at. That's what sucks about being four hours away. I'm going to Beaufort next weekend to have dinner with his parents and go to a party and meet his friends."

"If you get a chance next weekend, then just talk to him—it can't hurt to just come right out and tell him how you feel. When you see him, just do whatever feels right." We both dig into our ice cream, my thoughts on Joe.

"Oh, I forgot to tell you." I tell my dad about Hailey's sister, but I don't tell him about Hailey being in rehab because I'd be no better than her if I shared. I do tell him that she's on an extended vacation, though.

We finish our ice cream, and then I take my leave, promising to come over for dinner.

***

I'm just pouring a cup of coffee when my front door opens. Carter, followed by Kyle, Robby, and Eli enter my house per usual. Carter's got a key and he's been known to just let himself in. Who am I kidding—Eli made a copy of Carter's key and walks in whenever he wants, too.

Kyle and Robby are cousins and look a lot alike; their dark hair is shaved close to their scalps, and they have the same hazel eyes. They're both tall and lean, and their only difference is Kyle's skin tone is dark olive and Robby's is more peaches and cream. They're Carter's age, and they all went to school together.

Growing up with one little brother and three pseudo-little brothers made it hard to date or have friends over because those assholes would torment us relentlessly. My brother isn't a huge talker, especially around people who aren't family, but he got the other three to go along with whatever he planned.

"What's up, boys? I'm surprised to see you all up so early on a Saturday. Except for you, Kyle—how are Jenny and Jayson? I need to go visit." He's the only member of our band that is married, and his son is two. He's a terror, but he's cute so I can sometimes forgive him.

Kyle comes forward and kisses my cheek. "Yeah, little man was up at five this morning. I let Jenny sleep and got up with him. They're great, though, and I know Jenny would love to see you."

"What are you guys doing here? It's not that I'm not happy to see you, but I was just curious."

"We were on our way to have breakfast and wanted to see if you wanted to join us," Eli says, smiling widely.

"Yeah, grab some coffee and give me ten minutes to get ready." They're all grabbing mugs when I leave the kitchen.

In the bathroom, I pull back my hair, wash my face, and put on a little bit of makeup. I take down my hair and brush it out before quickly braiding it. I race across the hall and throw on cut-off jean shorts and a black tank top. I shove my feet into my Nikes and then head back out into the living room where everyone is lounging on my furniture. Ragnar and Lagertha are curled up next to Carter.

"You are the only woman I know that can get ready in less than ten minutes," Robby says as they all stand up.

"That's because she loved hitting snooze when we were younger, and if she didn't want to miss the bus, she had to get ready quick," Carter says as I grab my purse, and we all head outside. They rode together, so I climb in my car and follow them to our favorite waffle house.

As soon as my car's in park, Eli's opening my door for me and helping me out. "You are glowing. Joe looks good on you. I'm sorry I haven't been very nice to him. No one is ever going to be good enough for you." He wraps his arm around my shoulders and kisses my temple.

I love my crazy, overprotective family.

Breakfast is a loud crazy affair, and luckily we're regulars so we don't bother other patrons. I smile at my brother from across the table. He returns it and looks at Kyle, who's shaking his head while he tells us about Jayson's latest shenanigans.

Just like me, my brother can't wait to have kids. One might think that because our real mom and dad lost custody of us that it might make us think twice about children. I want to have children because both of my dads taught us what it's like to be loved and cared for…I want to share that with my kids.

Carter feels the same. He doesn't date a whole lot, though. It's not like he shares his sex life with me because ewww…gross, but I don't think he's dated anyone in a long time. When we were younger, people just assumed he was gay because our dads are. I hated that he constantly had to defend himself because of it. Maybe that's why he doesn't date a lot.

We finish eating and make plans to have band practice a couple of nights during the coming week; Kyle got us a gig for the end of the month.

As we head outside, I hug all of the boys bye, and Carter then walks me to my car. He opens the door for me. "You okay?" I ask.

"Yeah, why?" He hates when I worry about him.

"I don't know. I guess just checking on you. I've been so wrapped up in my own shit lately that we haven't talked about you."

He pulls me into a hug. "Hey, you've had some serious stuff going on. There is seriously nothing going on with me. I'm pretty boring these days. If that changes, I'll let you know." He's such a good guy, and I hope he finds someone to love and someone who will love him like he deserves.

I kiss his cheek before climbing inside my car. He waves me off before jogging back to Robby's Explorer.

Once I'm home, I have nothing to do, so I clean my house from top to bottom. It takes me all afternoon, but everything is sparkling. Of course, as soon as my cats walk through the house, cat hair will be everywhere again.

Picking up my phone, I know it's too early to call Joe. He's working a split shift and won't be off until nine o'clock. We have plans to watch a movie after that, and by watching a movie, I mean that we call each other, turn on the same movie at the same time, and comment on the flick.

It's actually a lot of fun, and usually we pick something that we've both seen but that we love. *Step Brothers* is on the agenda for later, and it's our favorite.

***

I laugh into the phone as Joe quotes the line from the movie where Will Ferrell and John C. Reilly decide they're best friends. "I miss you," I blurt out.

His chuckle warms me. "Awww…I miss you too, baby, but you'll be here next weekend. My mom and sisters are excited to see you. They want to steal you and take you to lunch Saturday. I hope that's okay; if it's too much, I can tell them you'll go out with them another time."

"No, that's fine. You mom and sisters are seriously sweet. So tell me about this party that you're taking me to." I'm nervous about hanging with his friends. They're all in their early twenties, and I'm in my early thirties…what could I possibly have in common with any of them?

"It's just some friends from high school. It'll be a good time, I promise." I don't completely believe that, but I'll go and hope I have a good time.

"I'm looking forward to meeting them. Umm…I have something to tell you." I've been dying to ask him about dancing.

"What?" he asks slowly.

"Oh God, that didn't sound right. I've seen a certain video of a certain someone dancing."

"I'm gonna kill Violet."

"No, don't. I wasn't supposed to tell, but you were so good."

"Thanks. Not many people other than family know about it. Violet asked me to do it, and I couldn't say no to her. Plus it was for our grandma."

"Do you still have the tap shoes and that fedora?"

He chuckles. "Mmmm…I might be able to find them. Are you going to be the dirty dance instructor?"

I feel my cheeks heat up. "Yeah, or maybe you're the dance instructor and I'm the naughty student who just can't get it right."

His answering groan makes me smile. "Oh baby, I like that so much better." He clears his throat. "What are you wearing?" His question throws me off guard.

"Um—I'm wearing a blue tank top and little white shorts. What are you wearing?"

"Basketball shorts and no shirt."

I moan because I can just picture how sexy he looks. "No shirt, huh? I don't believe you."

"Oh yeah? Give me two seconds." I hear a rustling sound. Then he gets back on. "Check on your phone."

I put him on speaker, pull up the text he just sent,

and groan. He's reclining on his bed with his free arm behind his head. His delicious muscles and tattoos are on display for me. "You know I don't think I've ever really looked at your tats. Next time I see you, I think I'm going to have to rectify that."

"You will and I'll let you. Now it's your turn. Send me a picture."

"Okay, give me a second." I get up, racing into the bathroom and looking at myself in the mirror. I don't look too shabby for having no makeup on. I quickly let my hair down and shake it out. It's totally sex hair, and I pull my tank top down a little to show off cleavage. I grab the hem and pull it up a little to show off my stomach.

A sharp pain hits me in the heart. I place my palm over my lower abdomen as a wave of sadness washes over me. Blinking rapidly, I stop the tears from falling. I take a deep breath and get myself under control. In front of the mirror, I put my hand on my hip, flash the rock 'n' roll devil horns, and stick out my tongue. Quickly, I snap the picture and send it to him.

"Just sent it," I tell him as I make my way back out to the living room.

"All right, I'm going to look at it."

I'm met with silence for a second. "What's wrong?" he asks.

I'm taken aback by his question. "W-What do you mean, what's wrong? Nothing's wrong."

"Baby, don't lie to me. Your eyes are very expressive, but good try trying to hide it with the tongue and the devil's horns. What's going on?"

He doesn't sound like he's going to let up about

it. "I just got sad for a second. I was pulling up my shirt, and my stomach's flat, and it just kind of hit me again why it is." The tears start to fall.

"Oh, Chloe, baby, I'm so fucking sorry. God, I wish I was there with you right now. You know what?"

"What?"

"I want you to lie down on your sofa. Make sure it's on your back." He's silent as I move until I'm lying flat on my back.

"Okay, I'm on my back."

"Good job, baby. Now I want you to close your eyes. Take some deep cleansing breaths in and out."

Doing what he says, I remember my breathing from when I tried meditation after my break up with Trevor. In through my nose, out through my mouth—I repeat it over and over and feel it begin to work.

"That's real good. That use to work on Abby when she'd have her panic attacks." His voice is soft and soothing. "Are you feeling better?"

"Yes, thanks. Sorry, I wasn't expecting that—it kind of hit me out of the blue."

"I know I didn't lose her like you did, and I can't understand what you're still going through, but—"

"You lost her, too. You're allowed to think about it and about her or what might have been. I'm sure we're going to think about her for the rest of our lives. For both of us, we'll learn to live with that little bit of pain we'll always feel. Sorry I ruined our date."

"Next time I see you, I'm going to spank your ass. You didn't ruin shit, and I don't want to hear you say that shit again."

Wow, he sounds really pissed at me right now. "I-I'm sorry."

"That's okay. Just don't ever feel like you can't share your fucking feelings with me. Even if things were to end with us, I would still want you to be able to share your feelings with me, especially about that."

I rub my hand over my chest because the thought of us not being together freaking hurts. "Okay, thank you, and the same goes for you."

We don't talk much longer after that because I have to work in the morning and he's got a playdate with his niece. I'm anxious to see him next weekend because I just want to let him hold me.

Chapter Fourteen

Joe

I tossed and turned all night. Every time I fell asleep, I dreamt of a raven-haired, blue-eyed little girl, and it ended the same way every time. I would be pushing her on the swing, and then she would just disappear.

I'm supposed to be over at Abby's around lunch time to spend some time with Natalie. Dragging my ass out of bed, I grumpily step into the kitchen to make some coffee. I grab my phone off the charger and send my cousin Carrington a text.

Joe: Hey cuz. Are you home this morning? Can I come over and talk to you and Damien?

With twins at home, I'm not surprised that she answers almost immediately.

Carrington: Hey you! Of course you can. I'm surprised you haven't wanted to talk sooner.

171

We'll see you soon?

I love my family.

Joe: Yeah let me shower and I'll be there in thirty.

Carrington: Okay. Come hungry I'm making biscuits and gravy.

After showering, brushing my teeth, and throwing on a t-shirt and basketball shorts, I slip a ball cap on my head and grab my keys.

Pulling up in front of their home a short time later, I climb out of my car as Damien steps outside with their daughter Shay on his hip. It makes me want to laugh because he's wearing a sleeveless tee, displaying his tattoo sleeves. He's got gauges in his ears, and his hair is a Mohawk—looking like a bonafide badass and his daughter has two tiny pigtails sticking out of the top of her head and is wearing a pink onesie with ruffles on the butt.

I shake my head as I reach him. "You are a sight, brother." He reaches out, taking my offered hand.

"Yeah, yeah, yeah. Don't even say it, I know."

As soon as I walk through the door, I'm hit by the delicious smell coming from the kitchen. "Babe, Joe's here."

Carrington comes out to greet me with their son Ryder in her arms. "Hey, honey. Breakfast is just about ready, and then I'll put the kids down for their nap so we can talk."

"Thanks, Care Bear. I appreciate you guys taking

the time."

We make our way to the dining room, and I watch as they move like a well-oiled machine. In no time at all, they have both kids in their high chairs with food on their trays. I help Damien bring out the food and set it on the table.

With full plates, we begin to dig in. "How are things with the DEA?"

"Busy, but I've been talking to your boss about taking a detective job they've been bugging me about." Damien was working undercover when he and Cari first met.

"What are you going to do?"

"Not sure yet, but some recent developments have me considering it." I look between both of them.

"I'm pregnant." I get up and pull Carrington into a hug.

"That's great news. I'm so happy for you guys." I let her go and then slap Damien on the back before taking my seat.

After breakfast, I help Damien clean up while Cari puts the kids down and closes the little gate, trapping them in the family room.

"I'll sit with the kids while you guys talk," Damien says. Cari kisses him, and then the two of us go sit on their back deck.

"How's Chloe doing since the miscarriage?" she asks. "How are *you* doing?"

I take a deep breath. "She's doing better. She has her moments, and I'm the same. How did you guys deal with it?"

"There's no real correct way to deal with

something like that. Mom and Dad were a great source of help while we dealt with it. I blamed myself at first—hell, Damien blamed himself too since I was unknowingly pregnant when all of that stuff went down at the strip club." She takes a drink of her tea. "Logically, I knew that wasn't the case, but you always feel like you need to put the blame somewhere."

"I dreamt of a little girl last night, one that looked like Chloe. Is that normal?"

"Absolutely, and again, it fades in time. I have to believe that things happen for a reason. I wouldn't have Ryder and Shay right now. I wouldn't have this baby." She places a hand over her stomach. "I still get nervous while I'm pregnant that I could lose the baby. I was the same way with the twins."

"Not that I want to hear about your sex life, but did you have trouble conceiving the twins or this one?"

"Not at all. We weren't even trying with the twins." I'm not sure why I asked. Well, maybe I do. I'm in love with Chloe. Shit, I think I've been in love with her for a while—I just haven't told her because I'm not sure that's how she feels about me. If I try to picture my future, I see her in it.

I know we haven't been together long, and hell, most of our relationship we've spent apart, but I know how I feel. *God, I hope she feels the same.*

***

Chloe should be here any time now. I can't fucking wait—to get ready, I went and bought new sheets for my bed, washed them, and put them on. I also bought some new towels since most of my mine were threadbare in spots.

I've cleaned my place top to bottom so she's not scared to stay here. My place isn't a pit by any means, but after being at Chloe's place that even with two cats was immaculate, I want to make sure my place is good enough for her. Her being comfortable is important to me.

My refrigerator is stocked with her favorite beverages. Her favorite snacks are in my cupboards. I even had my mom get me one of those diffusers like the one Chloe has, and I had her get several different scents. I'm nervous as fuck. We're having dinner at my parents' place tonight. I was hoping it could be just us with them, but Haddie will be there.

Abby wanted to come, but I didn't want to overwhelm Chloe, even though she's been around my family before. This is her first time coming as my girlfriend. *Wow*, I think that's the first time I referred to her as that. My thoughts are interrupted by a knock on the door.

I move quickly and pull it open. Chloe smiles widely and jumps at me, wrapping herself around me like a spider monkey. She smiles down at me before kissing my lips. It's short and sweet and ends far too soon. "I'm so glad you're here. I've been climbing the fucking walls."

"I broke several laws getting here, but my boyfriend's a cop, so I'm not worried." I chuckle and reluctantly set her down on her feet. She wraps her arms around my waist, resting her cheek against my chest. Neither of us says anything while I stroke my hand down her silky locks.

Her light floral scent makes me half hard, but I don't want her thinking this is the only reason why I wanted her here. I pull away enough to look down at her. "Fuck, I'm so glad you're here." Chloe's smile warms me in a way that terrifies me but leaves me feeling exhilarated and alive.

I bend down and kiss her softly on the lips. I take her bag from her and put it in my bedroom. Back in the living room, Chloe's looking at the only pictures I have on the wall. Most are of my nephews and niece, Cari's twins, and a picture of my brother and sisters—from when Abby graduated high school.

Coming up behind Chloe, I wrap my arms around her chest. She leans against me. "I can't get over how cute Abby and Ben's kids are. I know you said Abby isn't Natalie's biological mom, but she looks like her."

I lean in closely, and the more I look at the picture, the more I see it—from the matching dimples to their smiles and twinkling eyes. I place my lips against her temple. "You're right, baby. You should really tell Abby that. I know she'd be thrilled." I lead her to the sectional and sit down, maneuvering her until she's on my lap.

"How was your week?" This past week we haven't talked a whole lot because I picked up shifts so I could get this weekend covered and I could be off. I plan on spending every moment with her. Of course I do have to share her with my mom and sisters tomorrow, and my mom threatened to beat me if I encroached on their girl time.

"Busy with Hailey still on vacation. I worked

two sixteen-hour days while trying to get all the orders done so I could be off. Wednesday night I had to quit working on the bracelet I'm making because my hand started to cramp."

Whether she's at the jewelry store or at home, Chloe's always working on some piece. "My poor baby—maybe I'll just give your poor hands a rubdown later." She told me once that when she gets her nails done and they massage her hands, she embarrasses herself by moaning loudly.

She lays her head down on my shoulder. "Mmmmm…that sounds amazing. What time are we going to your parents' for dinner?"

"Dinner is at six thirty. Mom says bring your appetite." I lift her up and then stand. "Come on, let me show you around." I show her my apartment, and then hand in hand, we walk around my complex.

"This is really great. It's beautiful."

"Yeah, I like it. It's nice that Abby's able to bring the kids over to swim occasionally. I use the gym a lot, especially if the weather's bad, and the big selling point was the ability to rent a garage. I keep my bike in there and also use it as storage."

We make our way back inside, and Chloe excuses herself to freshen up in the bathroom so we can head over to my parents' house. I'm in my room changing when she comes in. She changed out of her jean shorts and t-shirt and put on a pair of tailored black shorts and a peasant top, the blue color matching her eyes.

Her makeup is light, and her hair hangs down her back in soft waves. She's barefoot and has the cutest, daintiest feet. "Do I look okay? I don't want them to think I was trying too hard."

"You look great." She kisses me quickly and then stuffs the clothes she was wearing into the bag she brought.

After I'm changed, we head toward my parents' place. Chloe's quiet as we make our way across town. Her leg bounces up and down, and she wrings her hands together. I place my hand on her leg to stop it from bouncing. "Why are you nervous? You know my parents."

She looks at me. "Well, this is the first time I've been to their place with us being together. Don't they think I'm too old for you?"

"Baby, my dad is a lot older than my mom. Age is nothing. They only want me happy, and Chloe, I *am* happy. Aren't you?"

Chloe pulls my hand up to her mouth and kisses it. "I'm happy. I just wish we lived closer together, that's all."

"Me too, baby."

We pull up in front of my parents' house and see my sister's minivan in the driveway. I look at Chloe and shake my head. "It was just supposed to be us, Mom, Dad, and Haddie. I'm gonna apologize right now because it's going to be chaos."

"It's really okay." I get out and go around to open her door and help her out. Hand in hand, we walk up to the door. I don't bother knocking—we just walk right in. Natalie greets us first...well, she greets Chloe first.

"Are you going to be my aunt? You look like Snow White. Can I sit by you?" My sweet niece fires off a barrage of questions.

"Natalie, leave Uncle Joe's girlfriend alone," my dad says as he walks toward us.

"Okay, Pawpaw." She gives us both a hug before scampering off to do who knows what.

"Chloe, it's good to see you again." My dad bends down and kisses her cheek.

"It's good to see you too, Dylan." He offers her his arm, and they walk farther into the house.

"Uhh…hello. Did you forget about me?" I holler from behind them.

Apparently Ben got called into work and my mom felt bad for my sister, so that's why she and the kids are over. It's really not that bad with them here—I was just hoping my parents could really get to know Chloe without any distractions. When I step into the family room, Chloe's hugging my mom and then Abby. They don't see it, but I do—Chloe smiles and reaches out, touching Abby's baby bump. She's smiling, but it's not reaching her eyes.

Luckily, Rion runs up to Chloe and wraps his chubby little arms around her leg. While still talking to Abby, she bends down and picks up my nephew in her arms. My mom comes toward me and gives me a hug.

"Hi, honey. Sorry about Abby and the kids being here."

I shake my head. "It's seriously okay. As you can see, she's enjoying the attention." Natalie's herding Chloe toward the sofa. Dalton comes toward me, and I pick him up, throwing him over my shoulder. I move farther into the room and sit down with Dalton in my lap next to Chloe.

After everyone sits for a bit, we all head into the dining room. My mom and Haddie carry out the dishes. It's chaotic until finally we get everyone's plates filled and the kids are finally quiet.

Conversation is light while everyone eats. Natalie is pretty much the one running the conversation right now. She's in kindergarten, smart as a whip, and loves school. We all listen as she regales us with tales from her class.

"For show and tell, Matt brought his pet tarantula in, and when Ms. James saw it, she screamed and ran out of the room. Matt's mommy had to take it home so our teacher would come back in. It was so gross." She's not looking at any of us as she talks; she concentrates on her plate.

"What did you bring for show and tell?" I ask her.

Natalie finally looks up. "Mommy brought my tap shoes, and I showed them how I can dance." She pushes back her chair, stands up, and with a hand on her hip starts moving her little feet. She sits back down. "They all clapped and said I was a good dancer. Am I a good dancer, Uncle Joe?"

"You're the best little tap dancer I've ever seen."

She smiles so bright. I wrap my arm around her and give her a squeeze.

After dinner, Chloe, ignoring my mom's request to sit down, helps Haddie clear the table while my mom and Abby clean the kids up. Abby tells us goodbye and apologizes for intruding on our dinner. I open my mouth to tell her she wasn't, but Chloe beats me to it.

"I'm glad you were here and that I got to spend time getting to know your sweet kids." Abby hugs Chloe, then we all head outside. Haddie's going with her to help with the kids in the morning. I walk around to the driver's side and give my sister a hug.

"I love her for you, Joey," Abby whispers in my ear. She pulls back and gives me a big smile before climbing in her minivan. I open the door to the back and climb inside to give my niece and nephews hugs goodbye.

I shut the door and walk around the front to pull Chloe back against my chest. We wave as they take their leave. With my arm around her shoulders, we follow my parents back inside.

"Who wants coffee?" my mom asks.

My dad and I say yes, and so does Chloe. My girl follows my mom into the kitchen to help her get coffee. As soon as they disappear, my dad turns to me. "She's great, Joe. I know we've known her since she was a little girl, but she's really grown into a fine woman."

My dad saying that really means a lot. "I'm falling in love with her." I say it quietly so I know she doesn't hear me.

"That's great, son. You haven't been serious with anyone since Tracey. You seem really happy, but you guys live four hours away from each other. That may be fine for now, but it can't work forever. What are your long-term plans?"

To be honest, I've tried not to think about it, because I don't think she'd consider moving away from her parents, brother, and friends. Hell, we've only had one real date, but I know how I feel. I know every time I leave her, I get an ache in my belly and a pain in my chest.

"I don't know…we haven't really talked about that stuff yet. I was hoping with her here this weekend that we could. All I know is I that I want to be with her, and every time I leave her, I feel ill."

We don't get to finish our discussion because Chloe and my mom return, carrying a tray of coffee cups and cake. My girl sits next to me and hands me a plate with a piece of my mom's famous homemade chocolate cake.

While we eat, my mom drills Chloe about her jewelry designs, and they plot for Chloe to make a mother's necklace for Abby, waiting to add the charm for the baby girl she's carrying until after she's born.

I'm ready to be alone with my girl, so I stand up. "You're leaving already?" Of course that comes from my mom.

"Babe, I'm sure they want to be alone." My dad kisses her forehead while she pouts.

"Oh, fine."

Chloe tries to collect the dishes, but my mom tells her to leave them—she'll get them later. They walk us out. My dad slaps me on the shoulder and mouths, *Tell her how you feel*. I give him a chin lift and then hug my mom goodbye.

My dad hugs Chloe, and then my mom does the same. "We'll pick you up at noon tomorrow for lunch."

"Okay, that sounds good. Thank you again for dinner. It was delicious."

We climb in the car and head back toward my

place. "Sorry it was so chaotic tonight."

I feel her hand on my thigh, and my dick immediately gets hard. "It wasn't chaotic. It was fun. Your family's amazing…really." Lacing my fingers with hers, I bring her hand up to my mouth and kiss the back of it.

We roll up to the stoplight that just turned red. Grabbing Chloe by the back of her neck, I pull her head toward mine until my lips can reach hers. I can only kiss her for a second before the car behind us honks. Chloe laughs against my lips before pulling back.

Pulling into the parking lot, I park and then help her out. Hand in hand, we make our way inside my apartment. I kick the door shut and begin to stalk my prey.

Chapter Fifteen

Chloe

The banging of the door has me whirling around. Joe begins stalking toward me with a hungry look in his eyes. My nipples harden, and I immediately get wet. I begin to back up, but he tells me to stop, and something in his tone has me freezing.

He reaches me and grabs several strands of my hair, letting them sift through his fingers. "You're such a good girl." A warm feeling spreads low in my belly as he drags his fingers down my neck to my collarbone. His finger dips down into my cleavage and then up the other side.

Joe's barely touching me, and I'm already so turned on. My body quakes as he slowly walks around me until his front is against my back. His hands are on my shoulders. I shiver as I feel his lips touch my ear. "Do you trust me?" Joe's words are barely a whisper.

I open my mouth to speak, but only a whimper escapes as he bites my earlobe.

"Answer me, baby. Do you trust me?" His tongue touches my neck, and I tilt my head to the side to give him better access.

"Yes, I trust you." It comes out as a moan.

"Good girl," he says against my neck. "Now I want you to go into my room, strip out of all of your clothes, and lie down on the middle of my bed."

I whimper as he steps back, missing the heat of his body. Turning to look at him, I swear my vagina quivers at the look in his eyes. I've never seen him look at me like this before.

"Go, Chloe." His tone tells me to do it.

I step inside his bedroom and strip out of my clothes until I'm completely naked. I crawl onto his bed and lie down in the middle as my heart beats a rapid staccato in my chest.

It feels like I'm waiting forever before I hear footsteps coming down the hall. My breathing speeds up until it comes out in rapid pants when he appears in the doorway.

"You're fucking beautiful." He moves until he's standing at the end of the bed. His eyes travel a lazy path from my toes all the way to my face. I watch him as he slowly takes his shirt off, licking my lips as I scan every inch of his lean, muscled chest.

My eyes follow his fingers as he slowly unbuttons his jeans, pulling them down with his boxer briefs. His hard cock bobs when it's freed from its confines. Once his clothes are completely off, he squats down and grabs something from the floor. As he crawls on the bed, spreading my legs, I see he's got handcuffs in his hand.

"Oh God," I whisper. My breasts get incredibly

heavy.

He sets them down on the mattress next to me and grabs my wrists, pulling my arms above my head. "Grab onto the bars." I do as he asks and feel the coolness of the steel as he clicks them first around one wrist and then the other. I pull on them, and they rattle around the spindles of his headboard.

"I've got the key right on the nightstand and can get you out of them really quick, okay?"

Can he tell my heart is racing? Is that why he said that? I nod my head, but he grabs me by the chin. "I need to hear that you're okay."

"I…I'm okay. I promise."

Joe brings his face down to mine, placing his lips on mine. I immediately open, my tongue seeking his. Our kiss is slow and lazy and oh so good, but he holds his body away from mine. Lifting my legs, I move to wrap them around his hips, but he lifts his body away from mine. I nip at his lip, and he pulls back. "Do I need to spank you?"

I shake my head because if he does I could possibly come right now. I've never been so turned on in my life, and he's not even touching me. He resumes our kiss, and then his lips start the path down my neck, licking and nipping at the sensitive skin while again holding himself away from me.

Joe moves south, kissing his way down my chest until he reaches one nipple and sucking it into his mouth. I moan, arching my back and pushing more into his mouth. He licks, sucks, and nips at it until I'm writhing beneath him.

He switches to the other, giving it the same treatment and causing my pussy to clench around the imaginary cock. A moan slips past my lips, and I wish he'd fuck me already. I'm mindless with lust, and I try to reach for him, forgetting for a second that my hands are cuffed. My hips thrust up, trying to come in contact with some part of his body.

Again his lips travel down my body, kissing and licking every inch of my skin. I whimper and cry as my clit throbs with the insane need to come. He reaches the apex of my thighs, and I want to whimper in relief, but the bastard doesn't go where I need him most. Instead, his tongue teases around my nether lips, and I jerk against the cuffs.

Joe lifts me up enough to slap my ass cheek, hard. "Hey! What was that for?"

"Quit jerking on the cuffs." His voice is low and commanding.

Lifting my head, I glare at him. "Are you trying to give me the female equivalent of blue balls?"

He chuckles, making me kick at him, but he grabs my legs and spreads them further apart and then slowly drags his tongue through my folds. My hips surge off the bed, and my back arches as I moan. Joe growls against my pussy and begins to attack it with vigor. His tongue flicks my clit over and over, and I moan as he pushes first one finger and then two inside of me.

I'm so wet that every time he finger fucks me, my body makes a wet squelching sound, but I can't even be embarrassed right now because I'm on the verge of coming and coming hard. He starts rubbing my G-spot, and pressure begins to build. I feel his lips wrap around my clit, and he begins to suck.

In no time at all, I'm coming and coming hard.

White spots cloud my vision as I cry out. I can feel him growl against me as he continues to lick and suck at me, prolonging my orgasm.

"No…more…" I pant, trying to wiggle myself away from his mouth.

He finally pulls away and begins kissing his way back up my body as I pant. My skin is coated in a fine sheen of sweat. Finally, Joe kisses my mouth, letting me taste myself on his lips and tongue.

Pulling away, he reaches into his nightstand and grabs a whole sleeve of condoms, ripping one off with his teeth. I watch with rapt attention as he quickly tears it open and slides it down his very hard dick. He reaches up and grabs my hands. "Hold on to the spindles and flip onto your stomach." It takes some maneuvering before I'm on my belly. He sticks a pillow under my head and arms. "Don't let go, baby—this is going to be rough, hard, and fast."

He pulls my hips up and thrusts inside of me. I cry out as he groans and buries himself deep inside me. Slowly, he eases out of me, and then he begins to move. He wasn't lying when he said it was going to be rough, hard, and fast because he begins to pound into me at a punishing pace.

His grip on my hips is sure to leave bruises, but I welcome the bite of pain. I feel myself hurtle toward coming again. My cries turn more urgent. I feel like I'm speaking in tongues, and I wish I could touch myself. "I need to come," I cry urgently.

Joe's front meets my back, and one hand reaches around and begins strumming my clit. "I'm going to come. Come with me, baby." He squeezes my clit between his fingers and thrusts deep, planting himself as he begins to come, me following behind him. My cries and his groans fill the room, and I feel his teeth clamp down on my neck. The sensation has me shaking and shuddering until my vision goes hazy.

I collapse on the mattress and am barely coherent when I feel him slip from my body and then move around. Next thing I know, I'm in his arms. "You okay?"

"Mmm…hmmm…I think you broke my brain," is all I can get out, and I feel his chest vibrate as he laughs.

"Are your wrists okay?" I feel him pick them up, inspecting them.

"They're fine." I burrow against his chest, tucking my face in his neck. His slightly sweaty, woodsy scent wraps around me as I feel myself fall asleep.

***

Today has already been a great day. First I woke up this morning to Joe kissing my neck and fingering my pussy. We made love, slowly, sweetly, and I came with a soft cry. I fell back asleep after we were finished and woke up to Joe bringing me toast and coffee in bed.

After we ate our toast and drank our coffee, we lay in bed talking. Twice I wanted to ask him what we were doing and what kind of future he saw, but I chickened out. What if he thought I was pushing him toward a more serious relationship than what he

189

wanted? Maybe at his friend's party and with a little liquid courage, I'll get the nerve to bring it up.

We worked out in the complex's gym for a while and then went back to his apartment, where we decided to shower separately because his mom was coming to pick me up in an hour, and had he showered with me, I would've been late.

Journey picks me up with the plan to meet Abby, Haddie, and Natalie at the mall. On the way there, Journey reaches across and grabs my hand.

"How are you doing?" I know by her tone what she means.

"I'm okay, as long as I don't think about it or her." Her hand spasms around mine, and I immediately feel bad.

"I'm sorry, Chloe. I shouldn't've asked. You don't need to answer me."

I squeeze her hand. "No, it's okay. Some days are harder than others, but it's easier when I'm with Joe."

"My son really cares about you, I can tell. He reminds me so much of his father. They have that intensity about them." It warms me to hear her say that.

"He's been great. Even when I tried pushing him away after I lost the baby, I said terrible things to him, implying that me losing her was what he wanted. I knew it was wrong as soon as it left my mouth, but I wanted him to hurt the way I was."

"Honey, I think that's totally normal after suffering the type of loss you did. He forgave you, so there's no point beating yourself up about it. Just move on and look toward the future."

Journey is right, and I've been trying to heal and plan for the future. It's getting easier and easier to move past it every day, but I know the pain will always live deep inside me. I'm confident that I'll be strong enough to live with it, though. "Thank you."

We pull into the parking lot of the mall and find Haddie, Abby, and Natalie waiting inside the door for us. Natalie breaks away from her mom and runs at Journey. "Gigi!" She talks her ear off about school, and Journey's attention is focused solely on her granddaughter.

Ugh…the sadness is trying to creep in, but luckily Haddie and Abby come toward me, and it immediately goes away.

Joe's sisters wind their arms through mine as we begin making our way through the mall. They all certainly make me feel like part of the family, and when we go to stores, they give me honest feedback as I try clothes on. For the party, I buy a pair of gray jeggings and a black flowy tank top with a blue cami to wear underneath.

Abby doesn't have very many nice things to say about some of Joe's friends when I tell them who we are going out with. I then tell them about meeting Chris in Atlanta and that he stared at my chest almost the whole time he talked to me.

After we finish shopping, we make our way across the parking lot to the gourmet burger joint we chose for lunch.

"Chloe, sit by me," Natalie says as we get seated at our table.

Pulling my chair out, I sit down next to Abby's

oldest. "Where are your brothers today?"

She smiles up at me with her gorgeous hazel eyes. "They're home with Daddy because they're naughty and they're boys. This is girl time."

I smile down at her as she begins to color and then look at Abby across the table with a raised brow. "They're not totally naughty—they're just three and two and are partners in crime," she says, "but that's what I get for having them close together."

Our waitress interrupts us when she comes to take our drink order, and as soon as she walks away, Natalie looks up at me. "Are you going to marry Uncle Joe? Can I be your flower girl? I hope you have girls...I don't want any more boys." She goes back to coloring, and I feel my face heat up as Journey and her two daughters smile widely at me.

I look anywhere but at them and am thankful that our waitress comes and takes our orders. When she walks away, I want to follow her, but I don't. Instead, I turn to Abby. "I hear you sing, too."

"I do but not too much these days except when I'm putting the kids to sleep, but I've always loved it."

"Mommy sings all the time. Gigi says Mommy sings like an angel," Natalie says from next to me. I wrap my arm around her little shoulders and give them a squeeze.

"I bet she does." Abby gives me a smile, and then I look at Joe's baby sister, Haddie. Over the years, she's really grown into a beautiful woman. She's taller than her sister and mom. She's willowy with long curly strawberry blonde hair and eyes the same color as Joe. She's also got a tiny gap between her front teeth just like her mom. She's stunning and doesn't wear a stitch of makeup. According to Joe, she's getting ready to begin nursing school.

"Haddie, do you have an area of nursing that interests you?"

She's sitting across from me. "Not really, but I think I want to do hospice. You know, helping someone at the end of their life. I know it'll be sad because I know they'll pass, but just helping them die comfortably and with dignity is important."

"That's amazing, and it's great that you know what part of nursing interests you. Your cousin Carrington is a nurse too, isn't she?"

"Yeah, she's a nurse in the emergency room. She actually works with Ben's mom, who's a nurse practitioner," Haddie says before picking up her iced tea and taking a huge drink.

The rest of lunch is good. We talk about their families and mine. They ask about my band and my brother.

"What was Joe like as a kid?" I look at Journey, and Abby starts laughing. "Oh God, do I want to even know?"

"He was a good boy, but he was mischievous. I used to get calls all the time because of him getting caught kissing girls. He shamelessly flirted with all the females, including faculty. I swear I spent more time at school for him alone compared to the other kids." Abby and Haddie both agree with their mom.

"Why can I totally picture him being like that?" I shake my head.

"He's definitely kept us on our toes, that's for

sure."

When the waitress brings the check, I try to hand her my credit card to pay for everyone, but Journey gives me a look that has me putting it away. Haddie takes Natalie to the bathroom, and we all make our way toward the entrance. "Abby, your belly is just so cute. When are you due?"

"March second." She rests her hand on her baby bump, and all I feel is envious. Our kids would've been close in age—Violet's, too. Fate is a cruel bitch sometimes. "Every baby I seem to show earlier and earlier."

I watch Journey put her hand on her daughter's belly. "I was the same way. You look beautiful, baby girl." It's times like these that I wish I had a mother. Don't get me wrong, I love my dads—I would die for them, and I would kill for them, but watching Abby and Journey share this moment makes me uncomfortably sad.

Without them seeing me, I slip out the door and stand outside, letting the warmth of the sun heat my skin.

"Chloe!" I turn to find Natalie running toward me. I wrap my arms around her as the rest of the women step outside.

A short while later, we pull into the parking lot of Joe's complex. I turn to Journey. "Thank you for a wonderful time today and a wonderful lunch."

"You're so welcome. I had a wonderful time getting to know you today." She reaches across and grabs me in a big hug. I don't know what comes over me, but tears leak from my eyes as I hug her back.

We finally pull away, and she reaches out, wiping my tears away. "No tears or Joe's never going to let me spend any more time with you."

I nod and give her a watery smile. "Thank you again for a wonderful time."

"You're welcome, sweet girl. Now go, because I'm sure any second Joe's going to come out here and want to know what kept you." I grab my bags and climb out, waving goodbye as she drives away.

I make my way up to Joe's door and knock. He gave me a key, but I don't feel comfortable using it. I'm wondering if he's even home when the door opens and he's pulling me inside. My bags quickly fall to the floor and are forgotten as he lifts me up, my legs wrapping around his hips.

His tongue enters my mouth, and I can taste the mintiness of his freshly brushed teeth. He pulls back and smiles up at me. "Both of my sisters texted me that they love you, and I'm sure my mom will do the same at some point. Did you have a good time?"

"I had a great time. They were all so sweet to me. So kissing all the girls when you were little, huh?"

He gives me that cocky smirk that I love. "What can I say? I've always loved the ladies."

I can only shake my head. Unfortunately, he sets me down. That's when I notice that he's freshly showered and wearing just a pair of black boxer briefs. "It's really not fair that you look this good in just your underwear." I walk toward his bedroom after picking up my bags.

As I lay the bags on his bed, I feel him come up behind me, wrapping his arms around my chest.

"Whatcha got in the bags?" He rests his chin on my shoulder.

"I got an outfit to wear tonight."

"I got a couple of steaks, a couple of potatoes, and some asparagus for dinner. I thought I'd make us dinner before we head out."

"Mmmm…that sounds great. Do you want any help?"

"Nope, you relax because it's going to be a long night. I know I didn't let you sleep too much last night." Just the mention of not too much sleep has me yawning.

He presses his lips to my neck. "Lie down, baby. I'll wake you in an hour."

I crawl onto his bed, and he covers me with the softest throw blanket I've ever felt. He bends down and kisses my forehead. I watch him walk out of the bedroom and close my eyes, immediately falling asleep.

Chapter Sixteen

I do one last flip of my hair, spraying it with hair spray and then flipping it back. I smooth out the flyaways and then grab my red lipstick out of my makeup bag. I swipe it across my lips and blot them before putting the cap back on. I look at myself in the mirror. "You're going to have a good time," I whisper to myself.

I figure if I repeat that to myself over and over, I'll start to believe it. My outfit looks good on me, making my breasts look bigger and my ass look high and tight. Hopefully Joe likes my outfit. I slip on a couple necklaces, a bracelet, and some rings. I step out into the hall and find Joe cleaning up the dinner dishes.

He's wearing a white t-shirt that molds to his lean muscled body and a pair of boot cut jeans that showcase his nice ass and the impressive bulge he has in the front. He's got a pair of black Nikes on his feet. I won't lie—he looks so fucking gorgeous.

When Joe turns toward me, his eyes scan my body, stopping at my face. "Damn, baby, you look incredible. Make sure you stick by me tonight…I don't want to have to beat asses if some asshole tries to fuck with you."

Moving toward him, I stop when we're almost touching. I place my hands on his chest and inhale his familiar, warm woodsy scent. "You don't look so bad yourself."

"You ready to go?" I nod, and he grabs my hand and my car keys and heads outside. He opens the passenger door for me, and I buckle my seatbelt and watch him as he moves around the front end and then climbs in the driver's side.

I watch as he adjusts the seat for his long legs, and then we make our way toward a little subdivision. There's a bunch of cars lining the street and people milling around the huge yard next to a beautiful ranch home.

I meet Joe on the sidewalk, and hand in hand, we walk toward the house. This is reminiscent of the last house party I was at—the day I lost our baby. As quickly as those thoughts arise, I push them away. Now's not the time to think about such things.

We step into the house without knocking since the door is propped open. People stop Joe, and he introduces me. I've met so many people I can't keep names straight. He grabs us a couple of beers. With his arm around mine, we head out French doors in the dining room.

His friend Chris sees us and waves us over. "Don't worry—I won't let him talk to your boobs." I laugh and bump my hip against his.

"What's up, brother? Chloe, you're looking

mighty fine tonight. If you're looking for a real man to take care of you, you can always come to me, baby."

I shake my head, but Joe leans toward him. "Dude, that is never gonna fucking happen."

Chris throws his head back and starts to laugh. "Oh, how the mighty have fallen. You're gonna break some hearts tonight." Joe's friend turns to the crowd and hollers. "Ladies, it is with great sadness that I announce that Joe Carmichael is off the market."

My face heats up as every woman there turns and stares at us. They look disappointed, and when they turn to me, it's jealousy and something else…anger, maybe.

"Seriously, asshole?" Joe says, and all Chris does is shrug his shoulders.

I look up at Joe. "Should I be worried now? Am I possibly going to get stabbed or something tonight?"

"Baby, I'm a cop. I'll protect you."

"Whatever you say, Officer Playboy." I feel his hand slide down my back until he cups my ass and then gives it a swat.

Why does that turn me on? I've played a little bit before, and it was okay, but with Joe…with Joe it felt like so much more. He dominated me, and when he handcuffed me, I swear I almost came.

Joe leads me toward the back of the yard where there's a fire blazing. He introduces me to a few more guys that he grew up with. They all seem nice, but some of them just seem really immature. Two guys off to the side are making out with the same girl. There's a group of girls dirty dancing with each other while a bunch of guys stand around and watch.

I look at Joe, and he's oblivious to it, but he's obviously also oblivious to the fact that I'm uncomfortable. I'm no prude, but I was also never really wild, either. I won't lie: I was a good girl.

Joe leaves me to grab us another drink. I should've gone with him, but I don't want to seem like one of those needy girls that have to stay by her man's side. That's not me. Chris comes sauntering over as soon as Joe disappears.

"Hey, Chloe."

"Hey, Chris. Your place is gorgeous. As big as this yard is, I bet it takes you forever to mow it."

He smiles down at me, and it gives me an uneasy feeling. He doesn't hide the fact that he's perusing my body with his eyes. Chris surprises me, reaching out and grabbing a strand of my hair. He gives it a little tug. "This isn't my place—it's my parents'. They're out of town." He looks toward the house and then back at me. "Did Joe tell you about our parties?"

I shake my head. "What about your parties?"

He tugs on my hair, and I try to back away. "Have you ever had a threesome? Have you ever let two men inside your body at the same time?"

"Excuse me?"

"Joe and I like to share, and I would love to have a taste of you. Would you let me? Would you let me have a little taste?" My heart is racing, and an ugly feeling swirls in my belly.

"I don't think so, sorry."

"Well, that's too bad. I do have one question, though. How does it feel to know that your 'boyfriend' has fucked every single woman here tonight? Joe is the ultimate player, and I'm thinking you must have some sort of magical pussy to get him to claim you."

I'm mortified right now, and every instinct I have tells me to turn and walk away—from this place and from Joe. My eyes glance around, and I can't help but wonder if it's true. I knew he wasn't innocent, but I also wasn't expecting this. What the fuck do I do now?

I feel Joe walk up next to me, and I can't stop it when he wraps his arm around my waist and I stiffen. He notices, because he looks between Chris and me. "What's going on?"

I debate whether I should tell him or not, but Chris takes that decision from me. "Nothing, man. I was just telling her about how we used to fuck girls together all the time and I was hoping to get a taste of her magical pussy."

"Are you fucking kidding me right now? Why would you say that to her?" Joe gets in his face. "What's your fucking problem?" He leads me away from the asshole until we're off to the side by ourselves.

"I'm really sorry about that. He's drunk, and when he's drunk, he runs his mouth. What else did he say to you?"

Should I really tell him? Yes, I'm not going to protect that creep. "Well, he thought you'd want to share me with him since you guys do it all the time. He also informed me that you've fucked every girl here. Oh, and also that my magical pussy must be how I got the ultimate player to claim me."

He closes his eyes and tips his head back, but the one thing he doesn't do is deny that he's fucked every girl here. My stomach turns, and I'm not sure how to handle this. I've said it before—I know he's not innocent, and I'm not either, but I didn't realize the magnitude of his sexual history.

"I'm so fucking sorry. I should've warned you about him."

I really want to leave, but I can't do that—I can't be that girl who gets upset and leaves. Do all of the girls here think I'm a joke because he was a player? Do they think he's playing me?

"Is it true?"

"What?"

I don't want to ask, but I need to know. "Did you sleep with all of the girls here?" He looks at me. I'm not sure what that look's about, but I know the answer. Nausea fills my belly, and I'm not sure how to deal with this. "You did." I nod my head. "I need to go use the bathroom."

"Do you want me to go with?"

I shake my head. "I'll be fine on my own." I feel his eyes on me as I make my way inside. There's a line for the bathroom. I pull out my phone and scroll through my pictures, stopping on a selfie I took of Joe and me laying on the bed. I'm smiling at the camera, and Joe's kissing my forehead. That's the Joe I've fallen in love with. Not the player that slept with apparently everyone.

"You're here with Joe, right?" I turn, and a redhead is standing next to me in barely there shorts and a skimpy tank top with her boobs spilling out.

"Yes."

She smiles at me. "If you're down, I could join you guys tonight. I know he likes threeways, but I think it's been awhile since he's had one. I'm sure it's just like riding a bike, right?"

"Um…I'm not really down for a threesome, but if you're that interested in one, I'm sure the two of you could find a third, but it won't be me."

I step out of line, and as I walk away I hear her call out, "Your loss." I make it outside and find Joe with Chris, and they're surrounded by girls. A red haze fills my vision, but I don't do what I really want, and that's to rip the hair out of each of those slutty bimbos. Instead, I take a deep, calming breath and make my way toward them. Joe turns to me as I approach and moves closer.

"Are you okay?"

"Not really. I think I'm going to get an Uber and head back to your place. I've kind of lost the desire to party." He wraps his hand around my bicep and leads me to the side of the house.

"You know I wasn't innocent when we hooked up."

"Yes, Joe, I realize that, but I also didn't expect to have each and every conquest of yours thrown in my face. Since we've been here, I've been propositioned to have two separate threesomes with you and someone else. None of these girls will talk to me. Everyone is so young here I don't fit in."

I turn and start walking toward the front of the house. "Chloe, I'm sorry, okay? Chris is a dick sometimes, and I'm sorry. Yes, I slept around…a lot, but that doesn't change who I am with you and what we have. I can't change the past, but I'm not that guy anymore."

Joe grabs my hand and leads me toward his car. We're both silent on our way back to his apartment. I honestly don't know what's going to happen.

We reach his place, and he leads me to his door with a hand on my lower back. Once inside, I turn to look at him. "Maybe we're just not meant to make it." God, it hurts to even say it.

Joe moves toward me. "You don't fucking mean that."

"I don't, but dammit, I've never felt so utterly out of place somewhere before. Those girls were all younger, with better bodies than mine." He pisses me off by laughing at me. "What the fuck is so funny!"

"Baby, have you looked in the mirror? You're fucking gorgeous and have a better body than anyone I've seen. You were made for me, and I was made for you." He moves toward me. "I fucking love you, do you understand that? I. Love. You!"

"What did you just say?"

He grabs me with both hands by my hair, tipping my face up to look at him. "I'm in love with you. I don't care about any of those people. Yes, I was wild, but that all stopped the moment I met you."

Tears pool in my eyes. "I love you, too," I whisper. "I saw those girls around you earlier, and I've never been filled with such rage. I swear I was going to rip their heads off."

His head tips back, and he laughs and laughs hard. I hit him in the stomach before wrapping my arms around his waist. "I would've loved to have seen that. Hell, I bet Chris would've busted out the baby pool and filled it with Jell-O. You could've made it real interesting."

"Ugh, shut your face. That guy is so sleazy." I tip my head back as he bends down, kissing my lips slowly and thoroughly. "I love you, Joe," I say against his lips.

"I love you too, baby, and yes, Chris is a total sleazebag."

Chapter Seventeen

Joe

Chloe sleeps soundly next me, but I've been up for a while just watching her sleep like a creeper, but I can't help myself. She's just so fucking beautiful, and last night after the disaster that was Chris's party, we watched a movie until I couldn't stand it anymore and needed to be inside her.

She ended up riding me on the couch until she came hard, and then with my dick still buried inside her, I fucked her hard against the wall until I came so hard that I almost dropped her and blacked out. Round two happened in bed with her on her hands and knees and me with a tight grip on her hips. My poor baby passed right out after that.

I reach out and stroke her cheek, and she snuggles further into me. I want her to move in with me. *Wow*, I seriously want us to live together. Would she really move away from her family, though? They're all extremely close, but I'm close to my family, too. Would I consider moving to

Atlanta? I like working in a smaller police force. It's pretty sweet working with my brother-in-law, and it sounds like eventually Care Bear's husband will be working with us, too.

No, I'd have to consider it, moving. It would be extremely selfish of me to just expect her to move and not even consider doing it myself. I lean forward and kiss her softly on the lips before I slide slowly out of bed and throw on a pair of basketball shorts. I head out into the bathroom first, using it and brushing my teeth. Then in the kitchen, I make coffee and look through my cupboards.

I find some pancake mix and whip up a batch. While I've got them cooking, I slice up some strawberries. I'm flipping the first pancakes when I feel arms wrap around my middle. I rest my hand on top of hers. "Morning, baby. I was going to bring you breakfast in bed."

"I woke up, and you weren't there. Do you want some coffee?" I nod, and she grabs two mugs, filling them both and then handing me mine. She gets out the butter and syrup for the pancakes and grabs a couple sliced strawberries, popping one in her mouth before sticking one between my lips. I bend down and kiss her, and the sweet taste of the strawberries bursts on my tongue.

I plate our pancakes and carry them to the table. Chloe puts butter on hers, sprinkles sliced strawberries on top, and then drizzles syrup on them. "I'm probably going to head home before lunch time. I've got laundry to do, and I've got to get started on your sister's necklace." She looks down at her plate and then back up at me. "I don't want to go."

"I don't want you to go, either." I take a deep breath. "What if I said I wanted us to live together?"

Chloe doesn't say anything at first, and I'm wondering if maybe she hates the idea. "Really? Would we live here or Atlanta?"

"I don't know. I guess I figured if it was something that we both wanted that we could talk about it."

"Can I have some time to think about it?"

"Of course. I don't want you to feel like I'm pressuring you into anything. Take all the time you need."

She gets up from her seat and comes around, climbing into my lap. "I really like the idea of waking up with you every day."

It's not long after breakfast that she packs her bag up, and I walk her out to her car to head home.

I open her door for her, kiss her, and then hug her before letting her get in. "Call me when you get home. Be careful, and I love you."

"I will, and I love you too." She gives me a wave as she pulls out of the parking lot of my complex. I watch as her car disappears from sight and feel a knot form in my chest. Did I jump too soon when I asked her about living together? Fuck, I hope not, because that's the last thing I want to do. Scaring her off is not what I want.

I head back inside and clean up the breakfast dishes before going back to bed.

***

Chloe

My phone rings, and I don't need to pick it up to know who it is. I know this past week I've kept conversations short or I've avoided answering his calls at all. It happened on my way home from staying with him last weekend.

Yes, Saturday night started out great and then went a little bad, but then it got really, really good. The day I went home, I had been shocked when Joe had asked me about living together, but I'd also been sublimely happy.

It was when I'd been halfway home that the fear had taken over. I'd pulled over at a gas station as I sat in my car hyperventilating. I'm not sure what triggered it, because I honestly want to live with him. Maybe it was because the only other man I had ever lived with had been Trevor, and he'd betrayed me over and over again.

I don't think Joe would betray me, but what if he wanted someone his own age after a while? I'd be devastated, because the feelings I have for him are so much stronger than any I had for Trevor. Joe's hot, and by the looks of his dad, he's only going to get better looking with age. I'm going to age before he does. He won't want that, right?

By the time I had gotten home, I had convinced myself that maybe I just needed to keep this casual. I tried to convince myself that I could turn off the feelings I had for him. Instead of calling him like he asked, I sent him a quick text that I was home. I then lied and said I was lying down for a nap so he wouldn't call me.

I focused solely on my job, even avoiding my parents and my brother. They'd all suspect something was going on and would badger me until I finally told them, and then they would tell me I was stupid and I'd agree with them. At the jewelry store, I've been insanely busy since Hailey is still gone. I haven't heard how she's doing, but for her sake, I hope treatment is working.

Again, my phone rings and brings me out of my thoughts. I take a deep breath and pick it up. "Hey, you."

"Why are you avoiding me?" He sounds upset. "Don't tell me you're not, because I've hardly talked to you. Did I scare you?"

"Maybe this is something we should talk about in person," I tell him.

"Oh, we will." I hear my front door open and move through my house to find Joe standing there.

"Hey, what are you doing here?" I move toward him, but I stop because he's not smiling. He's wearing a troubled look, and his mouth is pinched tight. Butterflies take flight in my belly. My hands begin to tremble. Is he here to end things?

"What was it that freaked you out? Was it that I want us to live together? Is it because you can't get past the fact that I slept with a lot of women before you? Tell me, because you looked pretty fucking happy when I said I wanted us to live together. What changed, baby? What's got you spooked?"

"I'm older than you." He rolls his eyes at me. "That may sound like a stupid reason now, but what about ten or fifteen years down the road? I'm going to show signs of aging before you. What if you wanted someone your own age, with fewer wrinkles and no gray hair? Then what am I left with?"

"Chloe, you're reaching for stuff, and those are all what-ifs. Do I seem that superficial to you? I love you. I may only be twenty-four years old, but I know what I want, and it's you. It seems like you're just scared." He moves toward me. "Baby, what is it?"

I shake my head because I can't say what it is because I'm not really even sure I know. There's just a clawing feeling in my gut and a paralyzing fear. Joe blows out a breath.

"Goddamn, Chloe, don't do this. I love you. You love me."

"I do love you. I just need to think about stuff." I keep my hands clasped in front of me so I don't touch him, because if I do, then…well, I don't know what I'll do.

"You need to think about stuff?" He sounds defeated, and that's my fault. "Fine, I'll go. Know this, if you want this to work, if you want this to go somewhere, then it's up to you to make the next move, because I *know* what I want." He moves toward me and kisses my forehead. "I hope I hear from you soon."

Just like that, he's gone. I sit down right there on the floor, and the tears begin to fall. Ragnar and Lagertha come out, and both silently curl up next to me, offering me their support. I look at them. "What did I do?"

They both give me answering "Meows."

Later in the evening, I'm making myself a glass of chocolate milk when there's a knock on the door.

211

A part of me hopes that it's Joe, but the logical part of me knows it's not. With slow steps, I make it to the door and see that it's my pops.

He's always been able to read me like a book. I take a deep breath and open the door. "Hey, Dad. What are you doing here?"

"You've been avoiding us, so I thought I should do a surprise visit and see what's going on. Last weekend you were in Beaufort with Joe, weren't you?" I nod. "Did you have a good time?"

"I had a great time. He told me he loves me. He wants us to live together." I don't miss the way my dad's eyes widen.

"Do you want to live with him? Because I know you love him."

"I do love him, but I'm scared."

"Baby girl, what are you scared of? My girl has always been fearless."

I don't answer him right away because I really can't verbalize it. "I don't know. There's just this irrational fear that won't go away. It was only supposed to be a one-time thing with him."

"Sometimes things happen that we don't expect. You know when I met your dad I had just broken up with someone else, and of course at that time I was out only to my family because it still wasn't acceptable to be a gay man. I went out to eat with your uncle Gary, and he'd been talking me through my breakup. I felt eyes on me, and when I looked up, I found your dad watching me from across the room." I've heard this story before, but I've always loved it.

"The whole time we kept looking at each other,

and finally your uncle Gary looked at me pointedly and said, 'If you don't go talk to him, I'll do it for you, and you know that's not a good idea.' So I did. I got up and walked over to him, and that was all she wrote." Of course Dad tells it with a lot more flourish.

"The whole point of telling you the story is that I hadn't been expecting to meet someone that night, but had I not gone with your uncle, then I wouldn't have met Ian and we wouldn't have fallen in love. We wouldn't have gotten you and your brother."

My eyes well up with tears. Because what scares me becomes crystal clear. "Daddy, what if I can't give him babies? W…what if I keep having miscarriages? Oh God, what if that's not even what he wants with me?"

He wraps his arms around me. "Oh, honey. You're young and healthy, and your doctor said that they didn't see any problems. It's very possible to go on and have healthy babies after losing one. Didn't his aunt lose a baby, his cousin, too? They both went on to have children.

"If you and Joe are meant to have kids, you will, and it doesn't matter if you give birth to them, adopt them, or foster them. You will give them so much love that they won't care how they came to be yours. As far as I can tell, he wants everything with you. You can't be afraid of the what-ifs. You'll never be happy if you do that."

My dad makes me another glass of chocolate milk and doesn't stay much longer, giving me time to think.

As I lie in bed, I stare up at the ceiling. My

thoughts swirl around in my head as I stroke Laggie's soft fur. I grab my phone off my nightstand and scroll through all the pictures of Joe and me. We do look pretty perfect together. The last picture is when we were at his parents' house for dinner and I'd asked Haddie to take it. Joe and I are in profile and gazing at each other.

His eyes are soft, his smile breathtaking, and his hand is resting lightly on my cheek. I remember that moment because it was right after that he kissed me lightly on the lips. His sister's dreamy sigh had us pulling away and laughing.

I take a deep breath and pull up his name in my contacts and send him a text.

Chloe: Hey, I just wanted to make sure you got home okay. I'm sorry you had to drive here to get me to talk to you, but I'm glad you did. It got me thinking about things and then Pops stopped by and after talking to him I got some clarity. I have to work in the morning, but can I call you tomorrow night? I love you so much xoxo

I hit send and set my phone back on the nightstand and hope to hear from him.

Chapter Eighteen

Chloe

My eyes flutter open as the annoying sound of my alarm goes off. I hit snooze and flop back down and rub the sleep from my eyes. Last night comes back to me, and I quickly grab my phone and pull up my text messages and don't see one from Joe, and from the looks of it, he read it.

Sadness washes over me, because what if I blew it? Both cats jump up on the bed and give me good morning "Meows." I give them both morning scratches and snuggles before climbing out of bed and starting the coffee pot. While it's brewing, I pop some bread in the toaster and pour food in the cats' bowls.

I slather my piece of toast with almond butter and pour myself a cup of coffee. Leaning against the counter, I eat my toast and drink my coffee. Why didn't Joe respond to my text? Is something wrong with his phone? Did he get called into work early? Hell, maybe he's just mad at me and didn't want to answer me.

If he doesn't get back to me by tonight, I'll text him again. A thought dawns on me. Maybe this is a test to see if I'm serious, but Joe wouldn't play games like that, would he?

I push those thoughts away, because I have to get ready so I can get to work.

An hour later, I'm walking into Harmon's. I find Mr. Harmon polishing the cases per usual. "Good morning, Chloe."

"Good morning, Mr. Harmon. The cases are sparkling."

He chuckles and goes back to wiping them down. In the back, I set up my work station. Checking my calendar, I see that in a half hour I have a couple coming in to have wedding bands designed. In the consultation room, I set up the binders with different styles in it and some bands that they can try on.

In the break room, I grab a bottle of water and take a sip as I head out into the front. I begin to straighten up the jewelry in the cases. During the week, we're never super busy. We do most of our business on the weekends.

Throughout the day, I've kept checking my phone, but there have been no texts or calls from Joe. I'm hopeful that there's a good reason for it. I clean up my workstation and can't wait to get home, take a bubble bath, and drink a glass of wine. Then I'll call Joe, and hopefully he'll answer.

***

The sun illuminates my bathroom as I lie back in my bathtub. The scent of honeysuckle tickles my senses as I soak up the warmth of the sun through the window and warmth of the water. We had been very slow earlier, so Mr. Harmon had sent me home after he took his lunch break.

I grab my glass of Riesling and take a sip. The taste explodes on my tongue, and I let out a sigh. I set the glass back down and lie back in the water. In my bedroom, my cellphone is charging, and I can hear it ring. I close my eyes when it stops, but it starts ringing again. Sitting up, I pull the stopper out of the tub and stand up, grab my robe off the hook, and slip it on. I open the door and step into the hall when I hear pounding on my front door.

My heart starts racing as I move to the living room and to the front door. I see it's Dad and Pops. I throw the door open. "What's wrong?"

I step back as they enter the living room. They both get close to me, and I start to freak out. "Baby girl, you need to get dressed and pack a bag."

"Why? What's going on? Please, you're scaring me."

Dad puts both hands on my shoulders. "Joe's been shot. We need to get you to the hospital."

A weird buzzing sound fills my ears, my hands tremble, and my legs feel like they're going to give out on me. My dad wraps his arms around me. "Be strong, baby girl. Let's get you dressed." They lead me back into my room. I watch them pack me a bag and then lay out some clothes for me. "We'll be out in the hall. Hurry, okay?"

On autopilot, I get dressed. I don't even know

what I'm wearing right now, and I don't even care. In the hall, my pops waits for me and wraps his arm around my shoulders. "Eli's going to take care of the cats for you, and we've already called Mr. Harmon."

I nod my head, hearing him but not. Outside, my brother is leaning against our dad's Highlander. I step right into his arms, and he hugs me tight. "He's going to be okay, Chloe."

He helps me inside, and I get into the third row and wrap my arms around my knees. Dad gets in the back with me, and Carter rides up front with Pops. Dad grabs my hand in his. "How did you find out? What happened?" I croak.

"Stacy called me. She didn't want you to find out over the phone. It was a routine traffic stop. The guy pulled his gun and shot Joe twice."

The buzzing intensifies, and I feel the blood drain from my face. "I...Is he d...dead?"

"No, he's not, honey, but he's in surgery. He's lost a lot of blood, and it's not looking really good right now." He brings my hand up to his lips and gives it a kiss. "Stacy said she'd call and keep us posted, okay?"

I nod my head and then stare out the window, watching the passing scenery. My parents and Carter all talk quietly, but I don't listen to what they're saying. I just think about every moment I've spent with Joe, every phone call, every text, and every video chat. I think about the child we lost. I think about all the times we made love.

No tears fall, because I feel numb. I wrap my arms around myself because I'm so cold I'm shivering. Pops' phone rings, and Dad turns down the radio.

"Hey, Stacy." Silence. "Okay, we're two hours out." A pause. "Yeah, she's right here." He turns to me. "Stacy wants to talk to you."

With a trembling hand, I take the phone from him and hold it to my ear. "Tay Tay," I whisper.

"Hey, honey. He's still in surgery, and we haven't heard anything yet, but they told us his surgery could take a while. Just send good vibes and prayers his way, and we'll see you when you get here. I love you, sweetheart."

"I love you too, Tay Tay." I disconnect the call and hand the phone back to my dad. My gaze turns back out the window.

It seems like it takes forever before we're finally pulling into the parking lot of the hospital. I see Tay Tay and Dustin standing outside. I'd heard my dad say that they would be. The SUV is barely in park before I'm busting out through the door and running across the parking lot. I run right into Tay Tay's arms as the tears begin to fall. "Shh…honey. He's strong. If there is anyone who can pull through this, it's Joe."

Tay Tay and Dustin lead me inside with my family following close behind. When we reach the waiting room, I see that there are people everywhere—some wearing uniforms, most wearing street clothes. I spot Joe's parents and siblings sitting in the corner. Journey sees me and gets up.

I step into her embrace as a fresh wave of tears hits me. "Come sit, sweetheart." I sit next to

Journey, and she holds my hand tightly in hers. Silence surrounds us as we wait for word. Dad and Pops go grab coffee for everyone and an herbal tea for Abby.

The sliding doors open, and a man in scrubs comes walking toward us. "Officer Carmichael's family?" We all stand up, my dad wrapping his arms around me. "I'm Dr. Petri, and I'm the one who treated your son. I have good news for you. Both entry wounds had exit wounds, and no bullet fragments were left behind. He's got three broken ribs, and we had to put in a chest tube to drain the blood from his lungs.

"He's intubated right now to get more oxygen into his body, but they'll remove it as soon as he's awake. The bullet in his shoulder nicked the subclavian artery, but we were able to clamp it off. His clavicle is broken as well. We've got him in recovery right now, but as soon as we get him into the ICU, you can go visit him. Just know that he's heavily medicated, and we'll keep him like that overnight."

"How did this happen? He was wearing his vest, wasn't he?" Dylan says as he looks between the doctor and Ben, his son-in-law.

"He was, but they used armor-piercing bullets. Forensics examined the scene, and as soon as we get the report, we'll know more."

Dylan starts cussing and storms out of the waiting room. I watch as Dustin and Parker go after him. Abby and Haddie flank their mom as she begins to cry. I don't think—I just go to them and wrap my arms around all three of them.

It takes a half hour before Dylan, Dustin, and Parker come back. I don't miss the fact that Dylan's clearly been crying. He goes right to Journey and pulls her into his arms.

It's ten at night, and Journey sent Abby and Haddie home over an hour ago. Abby was dead on her feet, and Journey was worried about her and the baby. Haddie went with her to help with the kids because Journey would need to rest.

Parker's asleep in a chair in the corner, and my parents and brother left to go to sleep at the hotel. They tried to get me to leave, but I'm not going anywhere until I see that Joe is okay.

"Mr. and Mrs. Carmichael?" We stand up as the doctor comes out. "He's been moved to the ICU. He's still critical, and the next twenty-four hours are crucial, but I think we're going to see him make a full recovery."

We all tell him thank you and wait for the nurse to get us. Tears leak down my face, and I feel arms wrap around me. Looking up, I give Parker a watery smile.

A half hour later, they bring us down to the ICU waiting room. His parents and brother go first, and I sit on the sofa staring blankly at the wall. I just want him to be okay. I want to be able to tell him that I love him and that I want us to live together, and if he'll have me, I want to be the mother of his children.

Some might say it's too soon or we're not going to work, but I will fight for us until the day I die. He was meant for me, and I was meant for him.

"Chloe?" With a start, I turn and find Joe's dad

standing in the doorway. "You can come see him, but they want us quiet, and we can only visit for a few more minutes."

I slowly make my way toward him. With a hand at the small of my back, he leads me to Joe's room. I pause in the doorway. He's hooked up to machines that fill the room with a steady beep.

"Come on, honey. It's okay." Journey holds her hand out.

Moving farther into the room, I take Journey's hand as she pulls me toward the bed. When I'm right next to her, she wraps her arm around my waist. "Talk to him; hold his hand. We're going to give you a few minutes alone, okay?"

"Are you sure? I don't want to take away your time visiting with him."

She squeezes my waist. "We'll have plenty of time to visit him. We're going to wait out in the waiting room." They give me a smile and disappear out of the room.

Moving toward the bed, I pick up Joe's hand in mine. "Hey, baby. I don't think you can hear me, but I'm so sorry this happened to you. I just want you to open your eyes and give me the naughty smirk of yours, but I know you need to heal. So you sleep...sleep until you're strong enough, and I'll be here waiting for you to wake up."

I bring his hand up to my lips, kissing it softly. Still holding his hand, I bend down and kiss his forehead. "I'll be right outside, baby." Walking backward, I can't and won't take my eyes off of him until I'm out the door.

On my way out to the waiting room, I say a little

prayer for healing and for him to wake up.

Chapter Nineteen

Joe

I've been in the hospital for a week and a half, and I'm ready to lose my fucking mind. I finally woke up the day after I got shot to find Chloe asleep, curled up in a chair in the corner of my room. I had pressed the call button, and after that it was nurses and a doctor coming in to check on me. It felt like someone had stomped on my chest, and it was hard taking deep breaths.

Chloe had been quiet, and then she disappeared while they were checking on me, but she returned with my sisters and brother when they were finished. After that, everyone came in and out until the pain was too much and they had me press the button to get some more pain meds, causing me to fall asleep immediately.

It was nighttime when I woke up again, and this time my mom and dad were sitting in my room. Mom fussed over me until finally Dad had to walk her out of the room. They returned a short time later, and my mom sat in the corner while my dad helped me get comfortable. Again the pain was too much, and after pressing the fancy little button, I fell asleep.

That's how things went for the first several days, and it wasn't until five days after the shooting that I could grin and bear the pain. My entire family has been here—even Violet flew home to see me for a couple of days before she had to go back. According to my dad, Chloe's been here every day. She left long enough to shower at my parents' place, but then she came right back.

The day I got shot, I noticed I had a text from her that I'd missed the night before, but I'd been running late and hadn't had the chance to respond to it. I knew she just needed time, and apparently she hadn't needed much since it was only several hours after I left that she'd texted me.

I was thrilled when the nurse took my damn catheter out. Nothing like having what looked like a rubber hose yanked from your dick. The worst was the day before yesterday when they finally removed the chest tube; luckily, they medicated me first. Four times a day, respiratory therapists have come in to give me breathing treatments and to check the numbers from some breathing test I've been made to do every hour.

They're worried about pneumonia, so I've been on IV antibiotics for the past week. Today, I have to have another chest X-ray, and as long as my lungs are still clear, I'll get to go home. It'll be at least six months before I'm able to go back to work…at least active duty, anyway. First, I'll have to have physical therapy for my shoulder, and then I'll need to speak to a specialist about being shot.

So far, I haven't had any issues, but they said it could happen anytime. There's no way I want to jeopardize my career or my future, so if I need help, I'll go get it. I'm not too proud to realize there may come a time when I'll need to talk about it.

A knock on my door has me looking up to find Chloe standing in the doorway. Every time she's been to see me, there's always been someone else there. This is the first time we've been alone. I hate how unsure she looks standing there. Raising my good hand, I wave her in. "Come here, baby."

She hustles toward me and grabs my outstretched hand. "How do you feel today?" Chloe reaches out and brushes my hair out of my face. I seriously need a haircut.

"Better. After they do the X-ray, they'll decide if I can go home or not." I let go of her hand and reach out, my fingers brushing over the skin under her eyes. "Have you gotten any good sleep?"

She smiles and shakes her head. "I'll sleep better once they release you. Your mom says they're getting a room ready for you there."

"No. I'm not going there. I love my mom, but she'll smother me, and that's not what I want."

"What do you want?" She sits down in the chair next to the bed, but I shake my head and pat the spot next to me. Chloe gingerly sits down, and I lace my fingers with hers.

"I want to go home but only if you're there."

"Done," she says but then starts to cry.

"Hey, hey, hey. Why are you crying?"

She wipes at the tears. "The last time I saw you, I had freaked out about us, and I thought maybe I blew it, and what if you didn't make it? I wouldn't have gotten the chance to tell you that I was sorry and that I love you, and if you'll have me, I want us to live together. I don't care if we live here, Atlanta, or somewhere totally new. You are my life now, and I realized that none of that other stuff matters. I just want to be with you."

I pull her carefully down until our lips are a hair's breadth apart. "I just want to be with you, too. I love you so fucking much." I kiss her lips hard, and she opens for me, my tongue dancing with hers. It isn't until we hear a throat clearing that I pull back and see that it's the radiology tech to take me for my chest X-ray.

Chloe helps me get into the wheelchair, which I fucking hate, but I could be dead right now, so I'm not going to complain. The tech gets ready to take me down. "Will you wait for me?"

She gives me that smile of hers that I love and bends down to kiss me. "I'd wait forever if I needed to."

As the tech pushes me out the door, he mutters, "You are a lucky man."

"No shit," I say and laugh as much as I can without being in pain. It feels good knowing that when I come back, my girl will be waiting for me, and I'll never forget how lucky I am.

***

Six Months Later

"Hey, baby, are you home?" I call out as I step into our apartment. The sound of her getting sick has me rushing toward the bathroom. As always, Ragnar and Lagertha stand guard.

So much has happened since I got released from the hospital six months ago. Chloe moved in with me to help take care of me while I recovered, and my whole plan was to get her moved in and never let her go again. She hated leaving her job, but her boss was a super nice guy and understood her reasons why.

Once I started therapy, the healing went much faster. Mentally, I only had a couple of instances where I lost it a little bit. That was when I had to face the asshole who shot me. Thank God for dashboard cameras, because it was an open-and-shut case. He was going away for a long time for attempted murder. Chloe was so strong while I dealt with all of that. She was patient and loving when I was moody and irritable. When I had nightmares, she would hold me until I was able to fall back asleep.

Oh, there were times where I tried to push her away, but she'd just ignore me and do her own thing.

My family absolutely loves her, but I don't blame them, because she's pretty fucking lovable. A couple of months ago, Abby and Violet both gave birth to healthy baby girls. Violet and Diego named their little one Luciana, or Lucy for short, and Abby and Ben named their little girl Paisley, or Pay Pay as we all like to call her.

Shortly after my niece was born, I'd finally been given the go ahead to resume sexual activities, and after Chloe and I talked and talked, we decided we didn't want to wait. She's now officially twelve weeks pregnant, and this weekend our families are getting together for a cookout where we plan on telling everyone. She's scared to do it because a part of her is still waiting to lose this baby.

Granted, I'm worried about that too, but I told her that we are going to just take it day by day. The cats both give me a "Meow" as I move them out of the way. Chloe is on the floor hunched over the toilet. I grab a washcloth, get it wet, and place it on the back of her neck.

I rub my hand up and down her back as she retches. "Were you able to keep anything down today?"

She nods her head, and I let out a breath. Last time, she had to have IV fluids because she got so sick. This time as soon as the test came back positive and the nausea started, we began the ginger pills. She sits back on the floor, and I take the washcloth from her neck and use it to wipe her face off. I then scoop her up in my arms and carry her into our bedroom.

After gently laying her down, I crawl in bed next to her, placing my hand on her lower stomach. I lean close. "Okay, little man—because yes, you're a boy; I can feel it. Let's stop making your momma sick. We need you both to stay nice and healthy." I bend down, kissing where my child rests, and pray that Chloe can make it through this pregnancy with no complications. She deserves that.

I feel her fingers spear my hair and her nails scraping my scalp. My dick twitches the way it always does when she touches me. Moving up the bed, I lie down next to her and pull her into my arms. "Are you feeling better?"

"Yeah, I'm just glad that most of the nausea is gone. This baby just hates the smell of hamburger, which sucks because I could really go for a bacon cheeseburger right now. I bought one on the way home from the store, and I had to throw it in the dumpster. That's why you found me puking." She snuggles in under my chin.

"I got my papers to return to active duty today." She's been apprehensive about me returning to active duty, but she supports me regardless. I've been itching to go back for the past two months, but my sergeant wouldn't let me until I completed my physical therapy entirely.

Chloe's dad Ian is a physical therapist, so when they'd come to see her, he'd always work with me, making sure my shoulder had good mobility. I've really grown to care about them and they for me. Even Eli's finally warmed up to me. Carter's the only one who has always seemed to be on my team.

"I know you've been ready for a while. Is it okay that I'm not looking forward to it?"

I lean back so I can see her face. "It's okay, baby, but you know I have to. It's in my blood."

"Of course it is. I'm sorry—you know I support you." She leans up, placing her lips on mine. With a laugh, she pulls back. "Sorry, I probably have puke breath."

I hug her to me. "I still love you even if you do smell." She slaps my back.

She doesn't know it, but I bought her a ring, and I'm going to propose at the cookout. I've been planning it for a while—I've just been waiting for the right time, and in front of our family and friends seems like the perfect time.

Chapter Twenty

Chloe

I climb out of our Jeep Cherokee, and Joe meets me on the sidewalk, holding out his hand. Lacing my fingers with his, I smile up at him. He cups my face with his free hand and kisses me slowly and thoroughly, just the way I like it. "I love you so much."

I cup his cheek and smile. "I love you, too." He puts his hand on my barely there bump.

"Okay, let's do this." Joe leads me around the side of his parents' house, and the backyard is full of people. Natalie, Dalton, Rion, Shay, and Ryder run past us screaming and laughing.

Journey notices us first and comes walking over with Paisley in her arms. "You guys are here. Chloe, you look beautiful." I kiss her cheek and then Pay Pay's forehead. Joe kisses her too and then steals the baby. He's going to make such a good daddy. I've never seen such a large man look so natural with a tiny baby in his arms.

Journey leads me around so I can say hi to everyone. His family is huge. I'm not sure how I'm going to keep some of these people straight, but I guess if I can remember all the kids, I can remember the adults. I spot my family up ahead. "Hey, guys! Did you have a good drive down?"

Dad kisses and hugs me first before Pops grabs me and pulls me into his arms. "We did. How are you doing? You look beautiful."

The prenatal vitamins I've been taking have done wonders for my hair. It's down past my bra strap now. Now that I'm hardly throwing up anymore, I'm starting to get that glow. "I'm doing great, and thank you. Joe got his paperwork to return to active duty. I'm trying to be strong, but I'm freaking out a little bit."

I turn and look behind me. Joe's standing with his brother-in-law, and he's still got the baby in his arms. "That's okay. I can imagine that you would be, but you just have to have faith."

"I know I do."

"He's a natural with that baby in his arms. Your dad says you're glowing. Is there something you want to tell me?" I hug my pops tight.

"Maybe."

His arms tighten around me. "Oh, honey. That makes me so incredibly happy."

"We're going to announce it tonight, so don't say anything." He nods, and I kiss his cheek before going to find my man.

***

Everyone sits around talking and listening to music. Joe is holding Rion in his lap, who is passed out. Dinner was delicious except when I had to sneak away to throw up when the scent of the burgers cooking hit me.

Ben takes his son from Joe's lap, and he signals for me to come to him. He stands up and wraps his arm around my waist.

"Everybody, can I have your attention for a minute?" A lot of people get quiet, but some are still talking, so Joe's dad hollers for everyone to zip it. "We're all together today, and I thought this would be a great time to share some news with you all. Chloe's twelve weeks pregnant."

He pulls me into a tight hug while everyone cheers and claps around us. "I knew it!" His mom rushes toward us and pulls me from his arms. "I'm so happy for you." She then hugs her son.

Everyone tries to come at us, but Joe holds his hands up. "Wait just one second. There's something that I've been meaning to ask you, Chloe." I watch in shock as Joe gets down on one knee in front of me. I cover my mouth as tears leak from my eyes as he opens a black box with the most beautiful ring I've ever seen.

"Chloe, I love you so much. I never expected to find someone who made me as happy as you have. We've had our ups and downs already, but they've made us stronger and have only solidified my feelings for you. You're going to be the mother of my child and any future children we're blessed with. Say you'll marry me, please." He slips the princess-cut solitaire on my finger as I nod and cry.

He stands up and grabs me, picking me up in his arms and kissing me hard. "Thank you," he whispers against my lips.

"For what?"

"For making me the happiest man on earth."

***

Joe groans against my neck as we both begin to come. "Oh God, baby." I grip his shoulders as he plants himself to the root, and I can feel the heat of his come as he explodes inside of me. He collapses on top of me, mindful of my belly.

All too soon, he pulls out of me and pulls me into his arms. I rest my hand on the puckered scar on his chest. My fingers swirl round and round as his hand slides up and down my arm. I tilt my head back, and I look at my future husband. I could kick myself for ever being scared. He's proven time and time again how much he loves me and how much he already loves our baby.

He's become the best partner I could ask for. I don't think I've ever had a more perfect day, and I can't wait to see what our future holds.

Epilogue

Joe

Six Months Later

Chloe grabs my hand in a punishing grip as another contraction hits her. She does this weird moaning thing that her midwife taught her. Why she wanted to do this natural is beyond me, but my girl is strong, that's for sure. She's been in labor for the past four hours, and about a half hour ago, they started getting a lot stronger, especially after her water broke.

"You're doing so good, baby," I tell her as she pants as the contraction ends. "Our boy is going to be here soon, and he'll be so excited to meet his momma."

"I can't wait," she cries and then cries out as another contraction hits her. "I have to push." Chloe moans as she again squeezes my hand.

Tara, the nurse that's been taking care of Chloe, comes in and checks her. She looks at us with a smile. "It's time to start pushing. Dad, grab her leg behind the knee. Chloe, I want you to bear down for the count of ten."

I grab Chloe behind her knee and wrap my other arm around her back. The nurse signals for my girl to start, and she's a trooper. She starts pushing and pushing, but it looks like nothing's happening.

I kiss Chloe's sweaty forehead as she cries.

"Come on, Chloe...give me a big push," the nurse says.

A scream rips from Chloe's throat. "It burns," she cries. I look down, and I can see the top of my son's head.

"Keep it up, baby. I can see his head." Chloe pants as she waits for the next contraction to hit.

The midwife, Mary, comes in and puts some gloves on. "Okay, Chloe, you're doing great. For this next contraction, I want you to push with all your might, okay?"

Chloe nods, and I bend down and kiss her lips. "You can do this, baby. We're going to meet our son soon."

The contraction hits, and she curls her body, bearing down. "Here comes the head, Dad," the nurse says, and I look down, and sure enough my son's head is coming out. "Chloe, give me another push."

All of a sudden, his head is out. The nurse suctions out his mouth and nose, and then my boy begins to cry.

"Okay, Chloe, one final push." Chloe pushes with all her might, and then my son slips free of her body. Mary lays him on Chloe's chest as the nurse starts wiping him off. My son screams his little head off, but it's the most beautiful sound I've ever heard.

I place my hand on his back and kiss Chloe's lips as she cries. Even though our son is covered in gunk, I still kiss his head. "He's so beautiful," Chloe says as tears roll down her cheeks.

"He is. We still need to decide on his name," I tell her as the nurse helps my boy latch on to Chloe's breast.

"I like Joseph Dylan Carmichael, Jr. What do you think?"

Tears fill my eyes. "I'd be honored for our son to have my name." I grab his little hand, and he wraps it around my finger, and my heart fucking melts. "What do you think, JJ? Do you like that?"

"JJ thinks it's great." Chloe begins to cry. "I…I'm s…so happy."

***

I'm sitting on the bed next to Chloe with JJ in my arms when her parents and mine come in. My mom, always the baby hog, takes JJ first. "He's so handsome. Hi, JJ, I'm your gigi, and I'm going to spoil you rotten. Chloe, he's beautiful. He looks just like his daddy did as a baby."

JJ gets passed around between the grandparents before the aunts and uncles come in and all hog him. Chloe falls asleep with her head on my shoulder, and my mom kicks everyone out so we can get some rest. I get her settled in bed and spread out on the little sofa bed. Our son is asleep in the little bassinet.

I've never felt this content in my entire life. I keep waiting to wake up from this dream. No one's life can be this perfect, but mine is.

***

Chloe

Two weeks later

I step out of the shower, dry off, and throw on my robe. With quick strokes, I brush out my hair and then quickly braid it. After brushing my teeth, I head down the hall into the living room. Joe is lying on the sofa with JJ asleep on his chest. "How was your shower?"

"It felt so good. It's amazing how much a shower can help. Do you want me to take him?"

"No, go lie down, take a nap. I'll come get you when he's up." I bend down and kiss his lips and the back of JJ's head.

"Thanks, baby." I head back down the hall and crawl into bed.

Once I'm settled in bed, Ragnar and Lagertha curl up in bed with me. The first time I slept with Joe, I never expected it to go anywhere. But not only did I fall in love with someone who became my best friend, but he's also given me the greatest gift of all.

I can't wait to see what our future holds, but all I know is that with Joe by my side, we can make it through anything.

***

Two years later, our son Hunter Garrett was born.

***

Two years after that, our daughter Clara Marie was born, and after that, I made Joe get a vasectomy or he was never touching me again. Our life is crazy and chaotic, but I couldn't be any happier than I am right now.

Our kids are healthy and happy and fill our lives with so much joy.

It had been a spur of the moment decision to go to Joe the night of Violet's wedding. Little did I know that one decision was going to change my life forever in ways I never expected, and every night I go to bed with Joe and/or one of our babies beside us, I feel a sense of contentment that warms me to my soul.

The End

Insta

Love

Book Five in the Love Stings Series

Coming Fall 2017

Chapter One

"Josie, are you going to go out with us tonight?" I turn toward Becca, one of the surgical techs I've made friends with since I've been here in Atlanta for my latest assignment. I'm a traveling nurse, which means I work at Brady Hospital for eight weeks in their OR before moving on to my next assignment. I'm already over halfway through this assignment.

I love doing it because I get to see different places and meet different people. It also doesn't hurt that I make a lot of money. I've got a substantial savings account that I'll eventually use to settle somewhere and buy a home. I just don't know if it'll be in Charleston, close to my family, or somewhere else.

My co-workers ask me to go out all the time, and I only say yes about half the time. I'm just a homebody, which is sad because I'm only twenty-eight. Hell, I can't remember the last time I went out on a date. I smile at Becca. "You know what? I think I am. Will you text me the details?"

"You bet. We're going to go see this amazing band. They haven't played around here lately since the lead singer moved away, but when she's in town they always perform."

I've always loved music. My uncle Cash plays in a band most weekends, and I love watching them, especially since my cousin Gavin, he and Aunt Tessa's oldest, started playing with them.

In the locker room, I change out of my scrubs and into my street clothes. I stop at the store before heading home, just grabbing a microwave dinner to eat before going out. *Shit*, do I even have anything to wear?

Once home, I pop my dinner in the microwave and go in the bathroom wash my face. I hear the microwave beep as I smooth moisturizer all over my face. I grab my pasta and scarf it down, leaning against the counter in the kitchen. I'm looking forward to getting out for a while tonight.

***

I look in the mirror. I added some curls to my light brown hair, showcasing the caramel highlights I had down two weeks ago. I kept my makeup light, giving my eyes a soft smoky look that my step-mom, Shannon, taught me how to do.

In my bedroom, I throw on a pair of black tailored shorts, a red short-sleeved fitted tee, and slip my feet into a pair of black sandals. I'd love to wear heels, but at five-foot-ten I tower over people when I wear them. Spraying a squirt of perfume in the air, I walk through it, another trick my step-mom taught me.

I grab my black clutch and stick my lip gloss, powder, license, and money in it. I lock my apartment door and head out to my car. The bar is called Holler's, and when I pull up, the parking lot is already full. I end up parking half a block down. Hopefully someone will be able to walk me to my car later.

I walk inside and find my co-workers around a couple of tables to the side of the stage. Becca comes rushing over. "Josie, you made it. Grab a glass—we've got a couple of pitchers."

I'm greeted by lots of smiling faces. When you take an assignment as a travel nurse, you never know what type of people you're going to run into. Most are super friendly and happy to have you, but occasionally you meet the ones that are assholes.

One of the nurses that works with us, Rob, fills a glass with beer and hands it to me. I thank him and take a generous sip. Becca moves toward me. "I'm so glad you came. You're going to love the band. They're great." She looks over my shoulder. "There they are."

I turn to see a woman who looks like a real-life Snow White with a gorgeous guy next to her who looks very familiar to me, but how do I know him? "That's her man," Becca says. "Her brother is the guy behind her."

The brother comes into view, and I swear my stomach does a little dip and my heart starts to race. His raven hair is short on the sides and a little longer on top. He's really tall, and from where I stand he's got the body of an athlete—lean muscles can be seen under his t-shirt and the jeans that are molded to his legs. I don't miss the tattoos sticking out from under his sleeves.

My eyes travel up to his face, and I see his eyes on me. I feel like I'm wired all of a sudden. Then he's moving toward me, and I turn fully toward him. He stops right in front of me. "Hey." His voice is deep and smooth and freaking sexy.

"Hi," I say, because I'm lame. He bites his lip and then flashes me a smile that makes my panties wet.

"I'm Carter."

"Josie. It's nice to meet you, Carter." When he grabs my offered hand, why does it feel like something amazing is about to happen?

Acknowledgements

First, thank you God for giving me the passion and ability to tell stories. I've treasured this gift so much, and I hope my readers can see that.

Thank you to my editor, Sydnee Thompson! We've worked well together, and you make my stories so much better and still keep the story the way I envisioned it.

Thanks to my PA Diane Plourde—you keep me on task and run my reader's group, review, and street teams brilliantly. You're too good to me and put up with my forgetfulness. I know I can come to you with anything and you always jump to help me.

I can't forget my ARC Team and Street Team. Thank you for loving my stories and wanting to be a part of the process. The reviewing and pimping means a lot!

To Deranged Doctor Design: Thank you for designing a gorgeous cover for me and always capturing my couples perfectly. I could honestly stare at it all day…Gorgeous!!

To my husband and boys: Thank you for putting up with me when I'm knee deep in my story, then edits and then promoting. Your love and support means so much to me, and I don't think I could do it without you and knowing that you all have my back.

Lastly, to Limitless Publishing: Thanks for taking a chance on a girl who just wanted to get her stories out there. Your support has meant the world.

About the Author

A Midwesterner and self-proclaimed nerd, Evan has been an avid reader most of her life, but five years ago got bit by the writing bug, and it quickly became her addiction, passion and therapy. When the voices in her head give it a rest, she can always be found with her e-reader in her hand. Some of her favorites include, Shayla Black, Jaci Burton, Madeline Sheehan and Jamie Mcguire. Evan finds a lot of her inspiration in music, so if you see her wearing her headphones you know she means business and is in the zone.

During the day Evan works for a large homecare agency and at night she's superwoman. She's a wife to Jim and a mom to Ethan and Evan, a cook, a tutor, a friend and a writer. How does she do it? She'll never tell.

Facebook:
https://www.facebook.com/pages/Evan-Grace/626268640762539

Twitter:
https://twitter.com/Evan76Grace

Website:
http://www.authorevangrace.com/

Goodreads:
https://www.goodreads.com/author/show/778844
4.Evan_Grace